A STRAY CAT

By Cheryl Campos

Copyright © 2016 by Cheryl Campos

All rights reserved. No part of this book may be reproduced or transmitted in any form or by any means, electronic or mechanical, including photocopying, recording, or by any information storage and retrieval system, without permission in writing from the copyright owner.

This is a work of fiction. Names, characters, places and incidents are the product of the author's imagination. Any resemblance to any actual persons, living or dead, or any events or locales is entirely coincidental.

ISBN# 9798688453256

Printed in the United States of America
By
GJ Publishing
Neilans.com
booksbyneilans@aol.com

ACKNOWLEDGEMENTS

Special thanks to Janice Bertrand and Carolyn Richards for their friendship, encouragement and their generous gifts of time and talent. I couldn't have finished the book without their honest criticisms and many positive contributions to the story line.

Every sinner has a future.

Every saint has a past.

CHAPTER 1

Evelyn had been in a tizzy all day, cleaning and cooking and getting everything ready for Mr. Weber and Miss Rose, who were coming home today after a month-long trip to the Andes Mountains in Chile. Every inch of the grand St. Charles Avenue mansion had been scrubbed and polished. Fresh flowers were in the great room. Evelyn had been Eric Weber's housekeeper ever since his college days. She wasn't a live-in back then; but now that her daughter was grown and her husband had passed away, she was very pleased to move with Mr. Weber to his new mansion and save on living expenses.

Otis the handyman was hired after the boss bought the mansion. He retired after years as a maintenance man at Dillard University, and did little odd jobs afterwards to keep busy. He took the job with Mr. Weber because his wife didn't want him underfoot all day. The money was good, and he particularly liked teaching Miss Rose about gardening. Otis worked all week before the boss' return to clean the grounds, weed the flower beds and have the cars washed.

As soon as the cab arrived, Otis ran out to get the luggage and bring everything upstairs. Evelyn met them at the door and welcomed them home. "Come and sit by the fire in the family room and rest for a minute. You must be exhausted. I put the cognac in there for you to warm up while I get supper on the table." The warm spring weather in Chile had been perfect. The cool damp air of November in New Orleans by contrast felt miserable.

"Something sure smells good," Rose said. "We were too tired to stop and eat and I'm starved."

"I made shrimp creole; and for you, Mr. Eric, I made your favorite Italian cream cake."

"Ahhh," he sighed. "God love you, Evelyn." Eric kicked off his shoes and stretched out his long legs on the ottoman in front of him. Eric was a tall and strong blonde and built like a bear. He was as well-known for his size as he was for his novels. Rose was petite and a drop-dead beautiful brunette. Whenever they appeared in public together, they caused a stir among men and women alike.

While they ate supper, Evelyn went upstairs to unpack the suitcases, put things away and take their clothes to the laundry room. Otis put away the suitcases and gear, then took their hiking boots out to the garage to be cleaned and shined.

The following day, Eric got to work outlining and organizing his notes for his twentieth book. The previous nineteen were all thrillers revolving around his fictional hero, Cade Monroe, and all became international best-sellers in five languages. Cade Monroe's next dangerous mission would be set in the Andes Mountains of Chile, so Eric's trip was for research.

Rose was his photographer and Spanish interpreter. Before Chile, she spoke only a few words of Spanish she learned from her Hispanic friends in the city. She picked it up quickly on the trip and was sounding like a native by the time they came home. Eric was surprised to find that she had a gift for languages. But Rose surprised him almost every day.

Rose was just seventeen when she came to live with Eric, but she was the most well-read person he had ever met and had an insatiable hunger to learn about everything. She was in her first year at Tulane University, going part-time to work around Eric's travel schedules, using the salary she earned working for Eric to pay her tuition. Since she lived in Eric's house and had no living expenses, she saved every penny she could for school. She postponed the fall semester to go with Eric to Chile, and was looking forward to going back to school in the spring.

Eric was gone from the house most of the time during November, attending a lot of meetings, he said. Rose didn't ask, but she sensed that something big was troubling him. He was distracted and had trouble working steadily on his book.

When it was finally finished, Rose asked if she could read the manuscript before Eric sent it to his editor. "I want to see how you used all the places we went and the photographs I took." He opened the pdf file for her.

"Oh, Eric! I just love the character of Athena," she said when she was finished reading. "She's wonderful. Why kill her off at the end? Cade really cared about her."

"Because Cade Monroe never stays with one woman," he said. "There's always a new hottie in every book. The good ones end up in bed with Cade and the bad ones go to jail or get killed."

"Athena was one of the bad girls," Rose said, "but I think Cade should spare her anyway. Athena could have killed Cade, but she never tried to when she had the chance. He admires her because she's his equal in intelligence and courage. He could let her escape from Interpol and come back in later books, over and over. He runs into her all over the world, but he always lets her escape because she fascinates him. Readers would love it, wondering if Cade and Athena would ever get together as lovers."

"I modeled Athena after you," Eric said with a sly smile.

"Me? And you killed her off? That's terrible!" Rose said indignantly. "Change it!"

"Okay," he laughed. "Cade will let Athena go free. Actually, I do like the idea of having her be a recurring character. I really didn't want to let her go."

"I don't want to let you go either. But it's time," he thought sadly.

CHAPTER 2

Eric struggled with himself for days until he finally knew it was what he had to do. "Rose," he announced one night over dinner, "I have some good news for you. You're fired."

She dropped her fork with a loud clatter. "You call that good news?"

"Yes, because I'm giving you a new job. A much better job. You are going to go to college full time, all expenses paid by me."

"What? Are you serious?" She was stunned. "That's so incredibly generous! Why would you do that for me?"

"Because I have more money than I'm likely to spend in my lifetime and you deserve a break. I had a free ride to Tulane and I would like for you to have one, too."

Eric explained that he set up a separate college fund for her at the bank, with enough to cover all expenses for her remaining time to complete her degree. His attorney would distribute the college funds to Rose as the tuition and fees came due, and her salary would be changed to monthly allowance payments from the attorney as well. His accountant would assist Rose in financial matters as needed.

To collect her allowance and money to pay for college, she would have to go in person to the attorney's office on the first business day of every month. She would have to bring proof of grades at the end of each semester and bills from school before any funds would be given to her.

"You go to the lawyer, not to me. And the money will be there for you as a guarantee, no matter what happens to me or between us. Nothing can take it away from you. It's yours as long as you stay in school. You are no longer my employee. You're being paid to go to college."

"Can I still travel with you on research trips? We have so much fun together and I'm constantly learning something new from you and the places we go. I'll study the language and be ready to serve as your interpreter."

"As long as it doesn't interfere with school, I would definitely like that," he said. "There are two more things you have to do."

"Anything you want," she gushed with enthusiasm.

"You have to live on campus and you have to join a sorority."

"You don't want me around anymore? You're pushing me away," she said sadly. "I understand that you're a bachelor and not used to having someone living in your house …"

"No, never! I'm giving you the freedom you need to be whatever you want to be."

Rose jumped up from the table with tears in her eyes. "You *are* pushing me away. This is the only home I have and you're putting me out again. You don't want me around!"

"No, you don't understand. This is *still* your home. Come home as often as you want to, but I won't always be here. I'll be travelling and writing again and I don't want you to be living here alone. You're going back to school and it would be very lonely for you rattling around in this big old house by yourself. I want you to take advantage of all the social life on campus and enjoy it. College isn't just about getting a diploma. It ought to be a bigger education than that. It's a full emersion experience you shouldn't miss."

"You'll be gone? Alright, no arguments," she said sniffing and drying her eyes. "Why do you want me to join a sorority? Those girls aren't likely to improve my education."

"They can, and a lot more. Just like you, I had no family when I was in college. No parents, brothers or sisters. My fraternity brothers became my lifelong family. I went home with them for holidays and took vacations with them. I stood in their weddings and grieved with them at funerals. I feel close to their wives and kids. After graduation, I helped out younger members who were still in school. They became like little brothers to me. My doctor, dentist, lawyer and accountant are all fraternity brothers."

"You want me to have a big family," Rose said, understanding and appreciating what he was offering. Eric nodded. "Okay," she said. "Where are you going for your next book?"

"I'll be in Israel for about a month, maybe more."

"While you're gone, I could take advantage of this palatial mansion, throw wild parties and invite some of your young fraternity brothers over for a weekend," she teased with a wink and a laugh.

"You'd better behave like a proper respectable young lady while I'm gone," he laughed and wagged his finger at her. "If you run amok, I will find out about it. I'm going to instruct my lawyer to whip your smart ass on the first of every month when you come to his office to collect your money."

"Okay, okay. I'll be a respectable woman, I promise; but, I'm missing you already," she sighed. "We have so much fun together. I'll miss beating you at chess," she smirked. "And you just started teaching me to play tennis and I haven't learned enough to beat you at that yet."

"Join the chess club at school and take the tennis class as an elective. And, by the way, you will *never* be strong enough to return my power serve when I turn it loose." He returned her smirk and flexed his biceps to emphasize the point. "You know you won't want to live with me after you finish school. You want to get married, have kids and have your own life. This is your time to spread your wings and fly solo."

Later that night, Rose thought about having sorority sisters as family. She remembered her late parents and how unhappy her childhood had been. "Tell me about your family, Eric," she said. "Parents and grandparents. Did they love you? Were they nice?"

"Why?"

Eric didn't know anything about her parents, just that they died. She never told him about any of her relatives, except a little about the grandmother she loved. "I'd like to hear about what it's like to live in a normal happy family. Were you happy when you lived at home?"

"Yes, very happy. We were a small family. I was an only child. My father was, too. We were very close to my father's parents. Grandpa Weber was a medical doctor and Dad was a lawyer. They both made a lot of money in their professions. We took nice family vacations. Grandpa taught me how to play poker. Mom and Grandma were housewives, loving and generous women, both very smart. They both loved to cook and bake. Our house smelled of something sweet baking in the oven every day when I got home from school. Mom played the piano at church and at home. She wanted me to take piano lessons, but I didn't care about anything but football from the time I learned to walk. I chose to go to Tulane so they could come to home games and watch me play. It was hard for them to travel as they got older. They died during my junior year."

"The piano in the great room. Was it your mother's?" Eric nodded. "Did your parents love each other and get along together?" she asked.

"Yes, very much. It was a happy home for all of us. It was as perfect a childhood as anyone could ever want. Like a fairy tale."

"You must have been very popular in school, being a big good-looking jock. Were you ever in love? Did you have a girlfriend?"

"When I was ten years old, a new girl transferred to my school. Anita was really cute and I was crazy in love with her. I sat next to her in the cafeteria at lunchtime. I asked her to be my girlfriend and gave her my pudding cup for dessert. She let me kiss her, but it ended when she started accepting lunch desserts from other boys. I figured they were kissing her, too. I was heartbroken. Once I became totally involved with football, I wasn't interested in having a steady girlfriend. But I was interested in getting laid as often as possible and dated as many girls as I could."

"That still appears to be your primary goal in life," she teased. "I'm glad you had a happy childhood. I didn't. I saw happy families on television but I didn't think there were any in real life," she said.

"Were you ever in love, Rose?"

"Well," she said thoughtfully, "it wasn't love, but I had a big crush on the boys' coach in eighth grade, my last year of Catholic school. Coach Vincent was young, probably right out of college. Not married and cute as he could be. I never felt attracted to boys my own age. Very Freudian, I suppose."

"You'll fall in love one day soon," Eric said. "You deserve to have a lot of love in your life."

Rose picked up her cat Precious. "My poor little kitty. Eric and I will be gone and you'll be here all alone. Evelyn will take care of you and I'll try to come home every weekend."

CHAPTER 3

Eric left for Israel two days before Rose's appointment to meet with the lawyer and collect her first check for allowance and expenses.

"It's time to get up, Miss Rose," Evelyn said, knocking on her bedroom door. "I have your breakfast ready. You don't want to be late."

Rose picked out her most conservative outfit, dabbed on a modest amount of makeup and went down to breakfast.

"Oh, you look wonderful," the housekeeper said. "Like you're a successful business woman already. Otis washed your car, got it gassed up and brought it around to the porte cochére for you."

Rose walked down the massive stone steps of the mansion to her convertible waiting outside on the brick driveway. The car wasn't actually hers; Eric got it for her to use while she was his employee. It was January and New Orleans was having a wonderful warm spell. The sky was bright blue and cloudless, so Rose drove with the top down.

January 6th, the Feast of the Epiphany, is called King's Day in New Orleans, and it marks the official start of the carnival season. The many

11

carnival krewe members were already busy with making costumes, hosting and attending parties, shopping for ball gowns and stocking up on plastic beads and other trinkets to throw from the floats. Eric always had great Mardi Gras parties at his house, but he would miss it all this year.

The law firm of Taggert, Anderson and Gregg, known in-house as TAG, and on the street as the biggest and best firm you could have on your side, occupied the top five floors of a modern office building downtown with panoramic views of New Orleans and the river.

Eric's attorney was a thirty-year-old hot shot on a rocket ride to the top. He attended Tulane and Harvard and was a member of Harvard Law Review. His specialty was business and finance. He was courted by big firms around the country, and probably could have clerked for a Supreme Court justice if he had applied for the job, but he was a New Orleans boy through and through and never considered working anywhere else. There wasn't enough money on earth to tempt him to leave his home town, family and friends. Besides, Jack was the type to blossom wherever he was planted.

Eric thought Jack would be a perfect mentor for Rose, who had the same major: business and finance. Eric and Jack were fraternity brothers and Eric had been a mentor to Jack as a young student at Tulane. It was Jack's turn to mentor now, and he couldn't refuse the assignment.

When Rose was escorted into John K. Monroe's office for the first time, he stood to greet her and swallowed hard. He was expecting a college girl, not someone like Rose. She was wearing six-inch heels and a plain, loosely fitted knit dress that would have looked prim and modest on most girls; but on that incredible body of hers, it was a killer.

Jack immediately understood the way Cade Monroe felt when he first saw Athena in Eric's last book, *Atacama*:

"It was easy to spot Athena. Her long dark hair hung over her shoulders in glossy loose curls, the way a little girl would wear it, unstyled, but not unkept. I wanted to put both hands in that lush hair and pull her face to mine. Like a great operative, she dressed simply to blend in to the crowd, but a burlap sack couldn't hide those curves. I'm supposed to stay close to her and find out what she's doing in Santiago. Interpol says she's as cunning and lethal as any operative they've ever pursued, but it will be my pleasure to stay right on top of her," he smirked. "She's a chameleon, her file said. Her face and expression can change from innocent virgin to temptress in a flash, so you wondered if you imagined it."

"Ms. Alvarez, I'm Jack Monroe," he said grinning and shaking his head in disbelief. She gave him a sweet questioning look. "You are exactly as Eric described you. You are Athena!" he laughed.

"But he wrote her character as a really bad girl," Rose said with a smile that made him salivate. A flash of the temptress, then the innocence again.

He invited her to sit. "Yes," he said with a disapproving look. "Eric told me you could be *challenging* to deal with, too."

She chuckled. "He must think you're up to the task." She gave him a hungry look and a flirtatious smile. That flash again.

He opened Rose's file folder, trying not to look at her. "This assignment is a first for me. My regular practice is business law, contracts and corporate finance. But Eric is a close friend and he wouldn't let me refuse. So this will be a learning process for both of us. Eric has asked me, as part of my responsibilities, to act *in loco parentis* on your behalf, even though you are no longer a minor. He told me that you are his godchild and you came to live with him after your parents passed away. He worried about leaving you all alone. I am to look after your interests and general wellbeing as a parent would, and not just hand you a check once a month. That's why Eric arranged it so that we had to meet in person. So we could talk and I could assure him that you are doing well."

"He sent me a copy of your grades from your freshman year. GPA of 4.0 straight through. Quite impressive. Your godfather is proud that you're doing so well, but he's concerned about your happiness as well."

Rose didn't hear a word he said. Yadda, yadda, yadda. Rose was busy sizing up her competition. Jack was in control of her money and she didn't like it. Remember the Golden Rule: He who has the gold makes the rules.

"Who is he? What are his weaknesses? He's quite good-looking and doesn't wear a wedding ring. There aren't any family pictures around. The office is large but conservatively decorated. He wears his black hair a bit long for a business lawyer, so he wants to look sexy and all business at the same time. Appears to be close to six feet, probably a nice body under that suit. Rich, smart and cute. He's got the world on a string. This will be a tough one …"

"Are you enjoying school? Making friends?" he asked, breaking her train of thought.

"Yes. My best friend last year was nice. She invited me to go with her to visit her family in Florida for a week. It was great. My sorority sisters are the best. Eric said they would become like real family to me, and he was right. I'm moving into the sorority house this semester. Eric kept close to you and his other fraternity brothers after college, and I plan to do the same. Eric promised to take me to Rome on spring break, so I'm learning to speak Italian to surprise him."

Rose was as open and charming as a school girl, and Jack was convinced he imagined the temptress. *"What a sweet kid,"* he thought.

He felt more relaxed. "Are you keeping in touch with Eric while he's in Israel?" Jack already knew the answer to that, because he stayed in contact with Eric, too.

"Yes, he calls when he can and I send him e-mails all the time. I send him selfies and pix of everything. He said my sorority sisters are hot and my male friends are gay. I told him I go out on dates, and I think he's afraid I'm sleeping around."

"Are you being … um … careful? Well, that is … I'm sorry … I don't mean to imply …"

Rose laughed. "It's okay to ask. The fact is, I'm not practicing any sex, safe or otherwise. College boys don't interest me. They're like puppies. Lots of energy, but no training. I'll wait for them to grow up. You're an older guy, Jack. You know what I'm talking about." That fleeting look again.

Being an older guy with training, he under-stood exactly what she was talking about and what she was doing. It was going to be difficult to keep her from manipulating him for three years. Eric warned him she would try. "This girl is smarter than both of us put together, Jack. Watch out. She'll have you wrapped around her little finger," he said.

Jack gave her the monthly allowance check. "I'm sorry that my time is limited today," he stood to shake her hand and escort her to the door. "I'll make sure we have more time to get acquainted next month. We won't meet here in my office. I'll buy you lunch at the student center sometime between classes. The first of next month is a Tuesday. Check your schedule and e-mail me the time when you can be there."

He couldn't wait to get her out of his office before he got a hard on and became completely unglued. When she turned to walk away, he got weak in the knees.

Her knit dress caressed her magnificent ass, and walking in high heels made her hips sway like she was waving a red cape at a bull. Jack was the bull, ready to charge after her. *"Good God, what's the matter with me?"* he thought to himself with dismay. *"She turned me on like I was a horny teenager."* He took off his coat, loosened his tie and flopped into his chair.

As Rose walked out of the office suite, every male head turned to watch her go. Jack's client, Norbert "Wizard" Laurent, was among them. He dropped in unannounced hoping for a minute of Jack's time.

"Wow! Is that your new girlfriend, Jack?" He was still watching her walking away down the hall.

"No, she's a client. Come on in, Wizard, and tell me why you're here without an appointment."

"My friend, I'm here to make both of us even richer."

"Good God, Wizard! How many millions do you have already?"

"More than enough. But I have another bit of technical genius that I want to get patented, with half the profits going to my educational foundation. My wife wants me to double the endowment to educate more future scientists. Here's the information on the gadget," he said, handing over a big brown envelope. "I won't keep you any longer. Call me if you run into a snag."

Norbert Laurent got the nickname of Wizard in high school because he was a math and science geek. He got a full scholarship to MIT and worked as an engineer until he sold his first patent for mega millions at the age of twenty-three.

Jack handled Norbert's first patent and the creation of his foundation, and didn't expect to run into any problems. Norbert was introduced to Jack Monroe by Albert Melancon, a friend and client. Jack, Albert and Norbert all remained close friends over the years. Jack was the only one still single.

After Norbert left, Jack e-mailed Eric. "I met your godchild today," he wrote. "How could you do this to a fraternity brother and long-time friend? That child is going to make me CRAZY. You said she was challenging? What an understatement! I'm not sure I'm up to the task."

Eric e-mailed back. "Now you see why I put her in the sorority house and left the country! Hang in there, Little Brother. I need you to be strong and so does she."

He couldn't get her off his mind and was a wreck the rest of the day. He fantasized about taking her wildly right there on his desktop in front of God and everybody. Thank goodness his other clients were serious business people.

All of the monthly meetings with Rose after that were in public places, including her sorority house, restaurants and local coffee shops. He couldn't trust himself to be alone with her. Jack didn't live like a monk, of course. He dated cool society ladies, the types he met at expensive fund raisers or at the country club. They didn't turn him on just by walking into the room the way that Rose did.

Each time they met, it was harder for Jack to hide his feelings. Rose was seductive without ever trying, but sometimes, she *was* trying. Jack was the man in charge of her money, and that was reason enough for her to try to break down his resistance.

Eric stayed in Israel three months, then told Rose that he wasn't coming home right away. He was going to undisclosed locations throughout the Middle East. He had a limited opportunity to travel with American soldiers and research his next book, and would be home when he could. There would be no phone calls, but he would e-mail her regularly. He promised that they would meet in Rome in the summer instead of spring break.

Rose told him once that she wanted a traditional, respectable life of home, marriage and children. That's why he chose to match her up with John K. "Jack" Monroe. He was sure that Jack would fall in love with his Athena. They would be a great match. Like Rose, Jack was raised in the Catholic faith. He was nicely built and good looking, and at the perfect age to settle down and get married. He was a brilliant, successful lawyer and could afford a family. Jack was kind and sensible and would be a good husband and father. Eric didn't think highly of lawyers in general, but Jack was a truly good man in every respect.

Best of all, Jack Monroe was the kind of man who could stand up to Rose. Like the characters in his book *Atacama*, Cade and Athena, they were equal in strength and intelligence, and neither would get the best of the other.

CHAPTER 4

Rose and Jack met at the sorority house whenever it was raining. He was protective of her and worried that she would catch a cold or something. Rose thought it was sweet of him to be so considerate. The sorority sisters teased Rose about the sugar daddy who brought her a fat check every month and was obviously very interested in her. Rose tried to convince them about that *in loco parentis* thing, but they just laughed.

"He looks at you *loco*, but not very *parentis*," one told her.

Jack acted all serious and business-like, but the look in his eyes gave him away. He couldn't allow himself to get romantically involved with the girl he was supposed to be looking after for his friend and client, but his desire for her was undeniable. They started having their monthly meetings after work, so that he could spend more time with her.

Rose complained to Jack that her statistics class would ruin her GPA. "Pareto charts! Regression analysis! I hate it! Everybody in the class gets this stuff except me! They have the answers in class, but I don't even understand the questions!"

Jack did well in statistics when he was a student, so he tutored her twice a week to help her get through it. And to be close to her more often. The smell of her made him hungry like a wolf catching the scent of his prey.

"I could pay a tutor, Jack," Rose said. "You don't have to do this for me, although I do appreciate it."

"Why pay a tutor? Eric is already paying me a ridiculous amount of money to make sure you're doing well in school. I would feel personally responsible if you failed this class. I don't want the boss to fire me," he added with a chuckle.

Rose didn't purposely flirt with him during their sessions because she really needed his help. But flirting was as natural and unconscious to Rose as breathing. To Jack, it was erotic the way she sucked the tip of her index finger when she was concentrating. The way her face lit up when she finally understood. The way she parted her lips and studied him through her eyelashes when he was explaining something. The way her long hair fell around her face when she looked down at the textbook.

They met in the visiting room downstairs and the house mother noticed how their relationship changed over time. So did the sorority sisters.

"You aren't sleeping with any guys you date because you have the hots for that lawyer guy," her best friend Kim said. "Have you told him you're interested?"

"No, because I'm *not* interested," Rose said. "You know I meet with him because I have to. And I don't want to mess things up with him, because my godfather would have a fit. God knows what he would do!"

"I don't know about that," Kim disagreed. "A tall-dark-and-handsome Harvard lawyer, smart, rich and single. Uncle Eric should be *thrilled* for you to fall in love with a catch like that. Then he wouldn't have to support you anymore. My parents would be ecstatic if he were my boyfriend."

One evening while some of the girls were watching the *Titanic* video for the hundredth time, Rose thought to herself about the characters. *"Jack and Rose. Jack and Rose. He's Jack, and I'm Rose!"* She raised her eyebrows and considered it. *"Me and Jack as lovers?"*

Rose aced her statistics class and hugged Jack's neck when she brought him the grade at the end of the semester. Jack offered to treat her to a steak dinner to celebrate. At least that's what he said. That hug with her breasts pressing against his chest left him breathless.

Rose ran upstairs to change into a dress appropriate for a … what? Dinner date? *"Is this a date?"* she asked herself. *"Should I look hot? No. Wear something plain. Eric told me to act respectable."* She wore four inch heels, a cranberry red pencil skirt and matching turtleneck sweater. Very modest.

Jack finally realized that he was crazy in love with her when she came down to the visitor's room to join him. *"What a woman!"* he thought, trying not to grin like an idiot. *"That's the mother of my children."* Then he shook his head in dismay. *"God help me."*

For the following monthly meetings, Jack arranged his schedule so that they could always have dinner together. They talked about personal things, music and movies and friends. Sometimes they argued about philosophy, religion, politics and economic theories. Other times they complained about their heavy workloads and frustrations. When Jack started picking her up in his car rather than meeting at a restaurant, their relationship moved up to the next level. It was more intimate. They hugged hello and goodbye. Then they started lightly kissing on the cheek, like old friends. It wasn't a lawyer/client relationship anymore. It was personal. They tried to treat each other like brother and sister, but Jack was having trouble keeping it cool. And the more time they spent together, the more her sexual hunger for Jack increased.

Rose's sorority held a spring formal every year at a fancy venue somewhere in town, and she wanted to buy a gorgeous beaded dress for $989 she found at Dillard's. She made an appointment with Jack to ask for an advance on her allowance.

He refused. "You have to learn to budget your income, Rose. An advance on your allowance is like an adult taking out a loan or living on credit cards. A loan should be for an important reason."

"This *is* an important reason," she pouted. "I have a date with a senior who's really hot!"

"No. I'm sorry. Find a dress that's within your budget."

Rose shed a few tears and begged some more, but it didn't work. Jack was ready to give her money from his own wallet, but he stayed strong. She stormed out of his office and slammed his door behind her.

Jack sighed and shook his head with exasperation. *"How could I ever think about living with a stubborn woman like that?"* Thoughts of her kept coming back to him all day, distracting him from his work. He was jealous of a college boy. *"A hot date worthy of a thousand dollar party dress? If he's that special, maybe she plans to sleep with him."* Jack cancelled the rest of his appointments for the day and went home to sulk.

On the night of the spring formal, Jack followed Rose and her date into the parking garage next to the hotel hosting the dance, then watched them walk away and disappear into the elevator. He parked where he could see without being seen and settled himself down for a long stakeout. He came prepared with the latest best seller to read on his Kindle and a thermos of coffee. They would probably return no later than midnight and he would follow them out again. He would wait all night, if necessary.

"Love is a dangerous drug to be avoided at all costs," he said to himself. "I have completely lost my mind."

At 11:08, they returned. The young man looked like he had enjoyed a few drinks, but wasn't wasted. He held Rose closely around the waist to hold her steady and get her to his car. Jack couldn't tell if she was drunk or drugged, but action was called for either way. Rose was a vulnerable young woman and he wasn't going to let anything happen to her. "And she belongs to me, Pal," he said before getting out of his car.

After the young man put Rose in the car, he was surprised when he came face-to-face with Jack as they both walked around the back of the car.

"Pardon me," Jack said with a pleasant smile. "I didn't mean to surprise you, but I see that both you and Ms. Alvarez are little bit intoxicated. Would you like for me to call a cab for you?"

The young man took a step back to look him over. "You know Rose? Who are you? Are you a chaperone or something?"

"No, I'm Ms. Alvarez's security for the evening. I'm here to make sure she gets home safely," Jack said with nonchalance.

"Security? Rose has a body guard? Do you have some identification?"

"Yes," Jack said coolly, revealing the unloaded pistol in his shoulder holster. Jack had a concealed carry permit because he often worked late at his office downtown.

The look in the college boy's eyes turned from impatience to fear. "Is somebody trying to hurt her?"

"Not necessarily, but Ms. Alvarez is an important young woman and she has security with her at all times. We keep a discreet distance and blend in wherever she is; but tonight, I was concerned about your ability to drive. I'm sure Ms. Alvarez wouldn't want the night spoiled by her date getting stopped for a DUI. I have a thermos of coffee in my car if you'd like to take a moment before getting on the road."

"N-no. I'm fine," the stunned young man said. "You can go home now, okay?"

Jack turned serious and stepped close to the young man, trying to look intimidating. He hesitated for effect before speaking again. "I'll be following you back to the sorority house in case you or Ms. Alvarez should have any difficulty."

"Sorry, Boy, but you won't get lucky tonight," Jack congratulated himself.

The young man thought it best not to argue, as the bodyguard was a bigger man and he was armed. *"Private security?"* he thought. *"Her god-father has hired trained killers to protect her!"*

Rose's date nodded nervously and got in his car. Rose was conscious enough to notice that her date had been talking to someone behind the car. "Who wazat?" she mumbled, barely able to keep her eyes open.

"Some guy looking for directions."

After Rose was delivered safely back to the sorority house, Jack went home, fairly confident that the young man wouldn't ask Rose for a date again in his lifetime.

CHAPTER 5

$\mathbf{A}$t the end of Rose's sophomore year, she met Eric at the Leonardo da Vinci Airport in Fiumicino, about sixteen miles outside the city of Rome. It had once been a little fishing village on the coast, growing to become one of the busiest airport centers in Europe.

Despite the grueling twelve-hour flight, Rose was excitedly looking forward to seeing Eric. He had been writing faster than ever before, determined to keep his mind focused on nothing else wherever he travelled throughout Europe. He finished writing his next book *Galilee* and sent it to his publisher before meeting Rose.

Atacama had been a wildly popular novel, largely because of the high voltage interplay between Cade and Athena. Readers loved to see the hero falling for a woman at last. *Galilee* brought Athena back, still an international criminal, but she was more attracted to Cade than before. Eric hoped that *Galilee* would be his biggest seller yet, because it just might be his last one.

As soon as Rose saw him, she could tell that Eric was sick. His hug was weak, his kiss was brief and he didn't have his usual energy. He had completed a round of an experimental drug cocktail before coming to Rome, and although it seemed to be slowly working, the treatment left him drained and pale.

He lied to Rose. He said that he had the flu during the winter and it led to pneumonia, and he was still recuperating. "You know how it is with us old people," he teased. "We don't bounce back as fast as you young college kids do."

Rose begged him to come back to New Orleans with her and take a long rest, but he refused. "What? Come back to the miserable heat and humidity of New Orleans when I can bask in the sand on the Riviera? When you go back home, I'm going to France to write my next book."

"Then let me spend the summer with you in France," she pleaded.

"With you around, I wouldn't get any rest or any work done. Remember how we were on the beach in Chile?"

"Quit writing for the summer and let's get crazy on the beach again," she said. "The women go topless on the beach over there."

"A good enough reason to keep you away from it," he said. "If you went topless, I'd have to get the *gendarmes* to keep men away. You're dangerous fully clothed."

Rose got to show off her conversational Italian for Eric when they went sightseeing and shopping. At night, they sat on their balcony and enjoyed the glorious view of the city in lights below and the glowing Vatican dome rising above it all a short distance away.

"This is your junior year coming up," Eric said, sipping his Italian wine. "Pretty soon you'll have a real job and be on your way to the top. You'll be starting your independent life."

"When will you come back home?"

"I don't know." He hesitated for a while, trying to decide what to say. "Our time together has been the best I've ever had. But we both need to move on, Rose. I'm ready to go back to the life that was meant for me. Traveling and writing. There are so many places in the world I haven't seen yet. And you're ready to start the life that was meant for you. Marriage, home and children. You can have a successful career or anything else you want."

"No, Eric," she pleaded. "I miss you so much. You can't just go away. You are everything to me! You gave me a home. You saved my life," she said with tears in her eyes.

"And you saved mine," he said. Eric thought about all the years he contemplated suicide before Rose came into his life. He was planning to finally do it that night he came home early from Belize. But he was surprised to find Rose in his house when he arrived, and she changed everything.

CHAPTER 6

Jack Monroe wanted to meet at Eric's house when Rose returned from Rome.

"Why? It isn't the first of the month," she said.

"I have a present for you that can't wait."

Rose didn't feel like entertaining company. Eric was sicker than he was letting on, but he brushed off her concerns. *"He said he needed to move on, but I don't believe it. Oh, God! I don't think I'll ever see him again."*

Jack arrived carrying a hat box tied with a black satin ribbon. He escorted Rose to the family room, followed close behind by Precious, her cat. Rose sat in her favorite arm chair with Precious at her feet. Jack knelt down and put the hat box on the floor in front of her. He untied the satin ribbon and took out a small black and white Tuxedo kitten. His markings were almost identical to those on Precious.

"With Eric staying away so long and you living at school, I thought Precious would like some company. His name is Handsome. He's a little young for romance yet, but I hope that they'll get along and have a litter together one day." He handed the little ball of fuzz to Rose.

"Oh, he's so cute!" she said. Rose cuddled the new kitten to her face, thanked Jack and gave him a light kiss on the cheek. She put Handsome on the floor next to Precious so they could get to know each other. Handsome hissed at the larger feline. Jack laughed. "Give them time. We didn't get along very well at first either."

Rose felt so many different feelings at that moment. Gratitude mostly. But there was more. The irony of it. Eric didn't want her to keep a stray cat as a pet and demanded that she get rid of Precious. It was such a terrible night when they had the fight and he ordered her and her cat out of the house. But Jack is completely different. Did he know that she was heartbroken, that she might never see Eric again? Had he brought the kitten to try to ease her pain?

Affection. That's what she felt for Jack, and it surprised her. *"No, it's just loneliness."*

Rose knelt on the floor in front of Jack, and with tears of joy and sadness in her eyes, she put her arms around his neck. "Thank you," she whispered close to his lips. He hesitated, then slowly gave her his mouth. She kissed him gently twice, looked into his eyes and waited for Jack to take the lead. He caved in.

He took her in his arms, lowered both of them to the carpet and rolled his body over hers. His kiss was long, deep and passionate. She moaned and kissed him back thoroughly. Jack held her tight for a moment, struggling with himself to do the right thing. He got to his feet and pulled Rose to hers.

"I'm sorry I crossed the line there," he said, shaken with emotion. "Eric trusted me to look after your best interests. I'm sure that seducing his godchild isn't what he had in mind. I guess I should go."

Jack picked up the new kitten and gave him a hug. "You be a good boy, too, Handsome." He handed the little one to Rose and said goodnight. Precious wandered off toward the kitchen, no longer interested in the arranged marriage with Handsome.

Rose couldn't speak. She remained glued to the spot where he left her, watching him leave, savoring the kiss that she could still taste and pondering what all of it meant.

"He clearly wants to have sex, but maybe it's more than that. Could he feel real affection for me, or did he just react because I kissed him first? Was he really worried about what Eric would think, or did he just want to put some distance between us? Well, if the only thing he feels for me is lust, that's a start. He kissed like he had real promise as a lover."

CHAPTER 7

$\mathbf{E}$ric left Rome after Rose, but didn't go to the Riviera. He bought a small used sports car and travelled around the hills of northern Italy, thinking, reading and writing. He decided that, if his brain tumor started growing again, he wouldn't try any more treatments. The fight was getting to be too hard. If he had time to finish one more book, it would be his last. He would retire to some quiet little Italian village where nobody knew him. Mostly, he didn't want Rose to be around to watch him die. It was important that she always remember him as the legendary macho man the world knew him to be.

Looking for a quiet little hotel to spend the night, Eric was directed by a local man to a nearby old Benedictine monastery, which offered simple accommodations at a modest cost to those seeking spiritual peace. Mostly their guests were priests who were travelling through on the way to visit Rome.

Eric was offered a very simple room with a single bed, an antique dresser and one wooden chair. His one window looked out onto a central courtyard that was beautifully maintained by the monks themselves as a place for quiet meditation.

There was a small church at the far side of the courtyard where the monks and villagers attended services.

The evening meal was simple but filling. When the monks retired for evening prayers, Eric went out to the courtyard to walk around.

He stopped briefly to look at a large crucifix that stood in the gardens. A young Italian-looking man was sitting on a stone bench close by. Eric walked over to the young man, who looked pale and sickly. "Good evening," he said. "Are you a guest here, too?"

"Yes. I'm Gabe," he said in accented English, offering his hand. Eric shook it and sat next to him.

"I'm Eric. Are you travelling through to Rome?" Eric asked.

"No. I'm here to die," Gabe said very matter-of-factly. "This is a peaceful place. I love it here. I'll be here 'til the end," he said with a sweet smile. "The monks have an infirmary here for their sick and elderly brothers, and they give hospice care for guests as well as their own."

"How can you accept death so easily? I can't. I feel angry and cheated."

"It helps to talk to him about it," Gabe said, gesturing toward the cross. "Like me, Jesus knew all his life that he would die young, without wife and children. Like me, he asked a friend to look after his only family member when he was gone. Mine is a little sister. Jesus and I have much in common and he gives me peace."

****

While Rose finished her junior year of college, Eric stayed on at the monastery as a long term guest and wrote his last novel on his laptop computer in his little room. The quiet surroundings made it easy to concentrate and work quickly. He felt at peace, even when the latest scans showed that the tumor was growing again, rapidly this time. The book would be shorter and less thrilling than his earlier works. It would be for Rose, and he had to finish it before it was too late.

Jack Monroe e-mailed Eric. "Call me. We need to talk."

Eric phoned him immediately. "Is Rose okay?"

"Yeah, she's great. Doing great in school, enjoying her senior year. She misses you and I think she's beginning to suspect that you are seriously sick."

"So what's the problem?" Eric asked.

"I, uh, I'm asking your permission to marry Rose. I love her."

"Have you slept with her?"

"No, Eric, I swear! But I have to be honest. I want to and I think she does, too."

That was the best news and the worst news. He hoped that Jack would love her and take care of her, but it felt like a cold icepick in his heart at the same time. He missed her so much. "Well, that will be between the two of you to decide. I can't think of a better man for her. You have my blessing."

"You sound shaky, Eric. Are you getting treatments again?"

"No, but the latest scan shows that it slowed down again. Go figure. Fast, slow, stop, shrink. The doctors have never been able to predict what it'll do next. I'm shaky, but I'm still here. The monastery will let you know when it's over. Paul Andry did my will and I've asked him to be my executor. I don't want him to open succession until Rose graduates. If she agrees to marry you, I hope that you will wait until then as well. It's important for her to finish school."

Jack was choked up. "I will, I promise. And I will take good care of her. Have you finished your book yet?"

"Yes. I asked my publisher to send the first copies to you and Rose."

"What's it called?"

"*Athena Reborn.* It's about attempting to recreate the forty-foot statue of Athena in the Parthenon as it was originally. Cade and Athena will get together again and she'll be reformed from her life of crime because of her love for him. They'll live happily ever after, just the way the fans want."

"I can't wait to read it," Jack said.

CHAPTER 8

In the spring of Rose's final year at Tulane, she invited a houseful of sorority sisters to have a sleepover at Eric's house on a Saturday night. She e-mailed Eric for permission, and he did more than give the okay. He said to show his answer to Evelyn and have her put on a "hell of party" for the girls.

Eric also e-mailed Jack Monroe and asked him to do a surprise drop in and make sure the girls weren't tearing the place apart or sneaking in their boyfriends.

Since the girls were all in their night clothes when the doorbell rang, Evelyn went to answer the door. She sent the girls away from the door and closed the double doors between the great room and the foyer. She was surprised to greet Mr. Monroe. The music was so loud Jack could hardly hear her.

"If you'll wait one moment, I'll clear the great room until you and Rose can go in the front parlor and talk privately," she said. She left him in the foyer and went in to tell Rose and shoo the pajama-clad friends upstairs.

The girls refused to be shooed away. They all had a little too much to drink.

"Handsome Jack is here?" one asked with a squeal. That's what all the sorority sisters called him, partly because of the name he gave the kitten, and because he *was* handsome.

"Let's welcome him to the party!" another girl said, removing her bathrobe and slippers.

"Hell, yeah!" another shouted. Her long sleep shirt covered her panties, but just barely.

The girls pushed past Evelyn and pulled Handsome Jack inside. "Take off the coat and tie and relax. I'll get you a beer," another girl offered.

"NO! No beer! And it looks like you young ladies have had enough for tonight. Rose's godfather asked me to drop in and make sure you were behaving yourselves. What would your parents think if they saw you like this?"

"I have been a bad girl," the tipsy one in the sleep shirt said seductively. "You should give me a good *spanking*." Other girls squealed and laughed, offering to be next in line.

"We all should go to bed now. Would you come upstairs and tuck us in?"

"NO! Back off and behave. All of you," he said angrily, scowling at them like a proper father figure ought to do. "Rose, I would like to speak with you privately in the front parlor, please." He spoke to her gently. Evelyn again ordered all of the girls to go upstairs until Mr. Monroe left the house.

Jack and Rose went into the front parlor and sat down across from each other on the twin couches by the fireplace. Rose was modestly covered up, wearing a long green empire-style lounging dress she bought in Rome. Her hair was a mess, which Jack thought was incredibly sexy.

The two cats followed them in. Precious hopped up next to Jack on the leather couch. Rose picked up Handsome and held him on her lap.

"I apologize for my friends' behavior, Jack. They never act like that at the sorority house. I'm surprised and embarrassed."

"How much have you had to drink tonight?" he asked softly.

"I've been careful to drink slowly and eat food. Just two beers. I knew one person had to stay in control to keep this bunch from swinging on the chandeliers."

"I'm pleased that you thought of that, Rose. You're a good girl. But I'm going to stay here tonight in case you need me. I'm going to tell your friends that the party can go on all night if they want it to, but no more drinking. I'll stay here in the parlor, but I can hear if things get out of hand. And if any guest misbehaves, I'll call a cab and send her back to the dorm. Understand?"

"Yes, whatever you say," she said obediently.

"Ooo, I just love to see a man get all manly!" she thought. "He thinks he's needed here. Guys need to feel needed. Maybe I can make him feel needed some night when I'm here all alone. A damsel in distress, rescued by my brave hero. I like it that he thinks of me as a good girl, but I want him in my bed at the same time. How do good girls get laid?"

When all the girls had gone to sleep in their bedrooms for the night, Jack Monroe slipped out quietly and went home.

CHAPTER 9

A few weeks later, Rose saw a notice in the business section of the Times-Picayune that John K. "Jack" Monroe had been made a partner at TAG. She cut it out and posted it on the bulletin board in her room at school, then called Jack to congratulate him.

"Have you been out to celebrate?" she asked.

"We had a little party at the office to make the announcement and my parents are planning a little family get-together at home this weekend. But other than that, I've been too busy to celebrate. It's going to take a little while to hand off some of the workload to the little Minions," he laughed.

"Are you going to hand me off, too?"

"No, never! You are my favorite client," he said happily.

"In spite of the Girls Gone Wild party?" Rose asked.

"I was pretty disturbed by your friends' behavior at the party, but I have to admit that it was a real boost to my ego when they called me Handsome Jack. To a stuffy old guy like me, it was flattering."

"May I take you out to dinner tonight to celebrate? I'll even pick you up at work in my car."

"That would be great. Be there at seven?"

Rose arrived at TAG on time and was escorted to Jack's office. She looked around while waiting, checking out the photos and personal things he had displayed. When he came in, she asked him about the middle initial "K" on his many certificates on the walls.

"My middle name is Kincade. My father's name is John, too; so instead of John, the family called me Cade. Eric used to tell me in college that I would never amount to anything in life, but he would make me famous by naming his adventure hero after me. After the novels became popular, I got teased by everybody when I said my name was Cade Monroe. It was like saying 'My name is Bond, James Bond.' So when I went off to law school at Harvard, I dropped Cade and became Jack."

"This is no coincidence," Rose thought to herself. "Jack and Rose. He's Cade and I'm Athena. Eric wanted us to be together, because he's never coming back."

"Where would you like to eat tonight?" she asked when they got to her car.

"Bud's Broiler by City Park. I used to go there all the time when I was in school and I haven't been back since I started working for a living."

"I've never been there. What's your fav?"

"Cheeseburgers smothered in onions and smoke sauce! The best on earth. I can taste it already." Jack left his coat and tie in the car and rolled up his sleeves.

"It's good to see you so relaxed," she said as they waited for their order. He seemed younger in his old hangout. The beat up wooden tables and benches had been carved and ink inscribed with initials and hearts by young patrons for years. Jack showed her the table with his initials, JKM.

"This partnership means the world to me," he sighed. "I've worked so hard. I'm relieved that I made it while I'm still young enough to finally have a personal life," he said with a big grin.

"What kind of personal life are you planning? Travel, dating, hobbies, buying a beach house in Florida? You're going to be very well off, so you should be dreaming big."

"I'm already well off and have been for a long time. My big dreams aren't about getting more money, although that is pretty great. What I want now is another partnership. A personal one. I want to get married and have a home and kids," he said softly.

"Oh well. I'm not likely to get him in the sack if he's looking for a wife," she thought with some regret. "He's a nice guy looking for a nice girl of his own social level to be his partner in polite society."

"It shouldn't take you long to find the right one, Handsome Jack. You're a pretty great guy," she said. "A prize catch."

Jack kept remembering Rose in that soft green dress with her hair in disarray, like she had just crawled out of bed. He wanted to see her like that again, crawling out of *his* bed.

Rose played the juke box while they waited for their burgers. She agreed with Jack that the cheeseburgers were the best in the world. They both licked the amazing smoke sauce off their fingers and swabbed the drips off the burger wrapper with their French fries. When they left the burger place and returned to Rose's car, she didn't start the engine right away.

"Something wrong, Rose?"

"I … I think so," she said softly. "Eric is very sick and he isn't coming back home again, is he?"

Jack couldn't respond. He looked away, nodding his head.

Her eyes filled with tears and she could hardly get the words out. "Is he dying?"

Oh, God, he didn't want to be the one to tell her. But he couldn't hide it anymore. Jack nodded slowly.

CHAPTER 10

Their next monthly meeting was on a Friday night. They had dinner at the New Orleans Country Club where Jack was a member. Rose recognized Savannah Melancon dining across the room with her husband Wayne. She brought Jack over to say hello and introduce him.

Before they got to the table, Wayne Melancon waved at them. "Jack Monroe! It's good to see you again," Wayne said.

"You already know each other?" Rose asked.

"Yes," Jack said. "I lived next door to their son Albert and was a groomsman at his wedding. I've been trying to get him to play golf with me, but he's totally not interested. I went to his parties when he lived next to me, but since he and Sherry turned their apartment into their business office, I don't see much of him anymore."

"If ya'll like parties," Savannah said, "I'll send you an invitation to our next event at LeBlanc Plantation. Albert and Sherry always come home for a big party. They'll be happy to see you again."

Jack happily accepted, then he and Rose made their polite departure and went to their own table for dinner. Rose was delighted to see a new side of Jack, who was light, charming and debonair with Rose's friends.

"You're making friends in all the right places, Rose," Jack said. "Did you know the Melancons are probably the richest family in the state?"

"Yes, Eric told me. They've been his friends for the longest time. Aren't they nice people? What a coincidence that I knew the parents and you knew the son."

"I'll introduce you to Albert and Sherry," Jack said. "You will all love each other, I promise. And his sister Amy, too. She stayed at Al's condo whenever she needed to stay in town for one of her social events and she's great. Both Amy and her husband Wizard have charitable foundations and she runs them both. Beauty and brains, just like you. And she graduated from Tulane, so you two already have a lot in common."

Jack changed the subject after the waiter took their orders. He wanted to continue the other conversation that started at the burger place. "When I made partner, you said I should dream big. What about you, Rose? Are you dreaming big now that you're almost done with school?"

"My dreams aren't all that big. Eric gave me a life of luxury, but he taught me that I had to learn how to take care of myself and not become dependent again. I want to marry and have kids, but he didn't want me to just latch onto some guy to take care of me because I was afraid of being on my own. I want to know that I can get a good job and have some money in the bank first, before I marry and start a family. Maybe even have a house in my own name. I don't need to be rich. I just need to know that I can take care of myself and won't be homeless ever again."

"*Homeless, cold, scared, hungry,*" she remembered. "*Alone in the dark. Stealing food. Never knowing when I'd get caught. Rainy nights on the street.*"

"If you marry the right man, a successful man who loves you, he would never let you want for anything. You wouldn't have to wait years while you do it on your own."

"But the man who provides it could also take it away. A successful man could afford a really good divorce lawyer and I don't ever want to be afraid of that. Or what if he died and left me penniless to raise our children? You've never been poor, but still you wanted your security assured before you settle down, and so do I," she said.

"Damn! Why does she have to be so sensible?" he asked himself in frustration.

"Yes. That's very sensible. Many married women never imagine that someday they might have to support themselves and their children all on their own. I'm sure you get to see a lot of them working on your community project for school."

The university requires all students to do volunteer services in their chosen field of study before they can graduate. As a business major, Rose helped poor women create business plans to start a home-based business.

"Yes, it has been a real eye-opener for me," she said.

"I imagine you've had some good job offers by now," he returned to their earlier topic. "The Freeman School at Tulane always has recruiters around looking to scoop up the brightest and best graduates, like you."

Rose smiled at the compliment. "Whitney Bank, the Morial Convention Center and a few others have expressed interest. But I haven't decided which way to go yet and I haven't scheduled any interviews."

"Would you consider an offer from TAG? You would be a strong asset to our business team," he said. *"And I've got to keep you close to me,"* he thought.

"Seriously? What could I do at a law firm?"

"I'd like you to be my assistant and advisor on business matters of all kinds. All cases aren't strictly about the law. I could give you time to work on your MBA if you want one. I can top any salary and benefits you've been offered. Working side by side with a partner in a large firm would look good on your resume if you wanted to move up to something bigger someday. And you would be working for a really nice guy," he said with a boyish smile.

Rose smiled back. "Why are you making me such a generous offer, Jack? It almost sounds like you feel obligated to Eric to keep taking care of me."

"NO! Not at all! Don't sell yourself short, Rose. This isn't an offer of charity. You'll work hard and earn every penny. And I won't be taking you out to dinner anymore after you start working for me unless we're entertaining a client. Strictly business."

"Well then, Mr. Monroe, put the offer in writing and I'll let you know," she teased. They left the restaurant arm in arm, grinning from ear to ear.

Before they got in his car to leave, Jack took Rose in his arms and held her close. They were standing in the dark shadow of a giant old oak tree, shielded from the lights of the parking lot. She was surprised, but pleased. He leaned down to kiss her and she put her arms around his neck to pull him closer. She parted her lips and welcomed his kiss. And it was a *really* good one.

"I love you, Rose. I have tried for so long to hold back, but I can't any longer. I love you," he said as he continued to kiss her mouth and neck and shoulders. "I wanted to wait until our business relationship was finished before telling you how I feel. Oh, God, I love you so much and I want you. I want to make love with you tonight." He sounded like he was in anguish. He held her so tight she could hardly breathe, but she didn't want him to let go. She liked the hardness of his muscles and his arousal pressing against her body.

"I'm so glad, Jack. I want you, too," she said in a husky whisper. Rose desired Jack, but wasn't sure that she loved him. How can a girl learn what love is when she has never been loved by anyone in her life? "*Jack is ready to get married. Is that what he wants with me? He wouldn't, if he knew the real me. He can never know the real me.*"

Jack took her to his apartment downtown. Neither of them spoke on the way over or in the building elevator. Both knew this was going to change their relationship from now on.

Rose was worried that she would fall in love with Jack. He surely wouldn't want a "stray cat" like her for a wife, and when he found the right one, he would leave Rose. If she let herself love him, it would break her heart.

Jack was bothered that his desire for Rose had overcome his conscience and he was old enough to know better. Is this what Rose really wanted, or would she regret this tomorrow?

When they got to his apartment, he made no pretense that they were just going to have a social visit. He took her hand and slowly led her to his bedroom. "Are you sure this is what you want?" he asked as he put his arms around her waist.

"Yes, I'm sure," she said softly, looking up at him. "But I'm not on the pill," she said.

He smiled at her happily, assuming it meant that she was not sexually active. "Not a problem," he said, his eyes full of love.

"I'll step out of the room while you get undressed and into bed. Call me when you're ready." He kissed her cheek and went into the living room.

"Holy shit! Does he think I'm a virgin, too shy to undress in front of him? Is this a Doris Day movie, or what?" Rose covered her mouth trying not to laugh. "Well, who says virginity can't be a renewable resource?" she thought with a shrug. Remembering a song from the movie Grease, she whispered the words softly as she undressed. "Look at me, I'm Sandra Dee, lousy with virginity." She folded her clothes daintily on a chair, hopped into bed and modestly covered herself up with the sheet, trying her best to look virginal.

Rose thought about the look in Jack's eyes when he held her close. He was completely open, honest and vulnerable. When he found tonight that she wasn't a virgin, he might hate her for acting like one. She had to tell him the truth. Not the whole truth, of course.

Jack came back to his bedroom when she called him. He had already removed all of his clothes in the living room except for his slacks. This was the first time she had seen him with his black hair tussled, and he looked adorable. He had always been perfectly groomed, in perfectly tailored expensive suits and silk ties. He never dressed casually for their meetings. Rose was aroused by the sight of his half-naked body. He was still young, but no longer had the skinny build of youth. At thirty-five, he had reached his prime in height, weight and muscle mass. Straight broad shoulders, nicely muscled chest and arms, trim waist, no tattoos. She was eager to see more.

He turned off the light, removed the rest of his clothes and got under the covers with her.

"Jack, I have to tell you something important. I, uh, well … I'm not a virgin." Jack didn't react one way or the other. Rose couldn't look at him. "When I was fifteen …"

"Shhh," Jack whispered to her, putting his finger on her lips. "You and I don't have any past. We're together and we begin today." He turned her chin up to look into her eyes, so filled with fear that he would reject her. "This is our first time together, so we're virgins to each other, aren't we? You are the only woman who has ever been in my heart."

Jack's lovemaking was sweet, slow and gentle. She wanted him so much it was hard to wait and let Jack take his time. But it was worth the wait. He tasted every inch of her, brought her to ecstasy twice and didn't enter her until she was begging for him. "Now, now, now, oh please now, Jack."

When he did, they moaned "Oh, God!" at the same time. She was hot and wet for him, and he filled her up completely.

Later that night, Jack woke up alone in bed. He thought Rose went to the bathroom, but when she didn't come back to bed, he got up to look for her. She was sitting on the couch in his dark living room, watching the stormy night through the glass wall facing the river and downtown. The curtains were drawn all the way back so she could see it all. It was blowing hard and lightning lit up the sky. She was wearing Jack's shirt that he left on the couch the night before.

"Is something wrong, Rose?"

"No. Everything is wonderful," she said with a contented smile. "The storm woke me up. I like to watch it rain and listen to the thunder. It makes me glad that I'm not out in it."

"I'm never going to be out in a storm again as long as I live," she thought. "Huddling under any shelter I could find. Cold wet feet all night long. Never again. I'm going to have a degree and a good job and a place of my own."

She held out a hand to him. "Come and stay with me."

"Forever, if you'll let me," he said. He hugged up to her. "This is romantic. Let's watch every stormy night together. Stay where you are and I'll get us some wine."

Rose stayed the weekend with Jack and they returned to the bedroom often to make love day and night.

On Sunday night, he drove her back to her sorority house. "Jack," she said, "we can't be lovers and work in the same office. It would make things too complicated. I'm going to accept the offer from the convention center."

"Okay, don't work for me. Marry me! I don't want to be just your weekend boyfriend. I want us to be husband and wife. Together forever."

Rose was startled by his proposal. "You want to marry me? For real?"

"Of course! I love you, Rose. I didn't know how dull my life was until you came into it. You're my joy. I can't imagine my life without you. I want us to have a home and kids and everything."

"I, I don't know what to say. I need to be independent first. Are you willing to wait?"

"As long as it takes. Move in with me after graduation. You can work and save your whole paycheck until you feel secure. I love you so much I don't want to be away from you ever again."

"No. We need to slow down. I'm not ready for that yet. I think I'd like to go back home after graduation, at least for a while."

Jack reluctantly agreed, but he had no intention of backing off. He was going to marry her and that was that.

They spent as many weekends together as possible until the end of the school year, and Jack was at her side at every school social event and football game. He claimed her as his own publicly, so no other guys would make a move on her. He took her dancing, charmed her friends, bought her flowers and offered her a diamond engagement ring for Christmas. But she wouldn't accept the ring yet. She asked him to hold it for a while longer. She wasn't ready for that big step. Jack was patient. As long as he had her in his bed, he could wait.

Rose eventually let her passion and sexual appetite run wild with Jack, which surprised and pleased him. "You're so young, my angel. How did you learn so much about making love?"

"Uh oh," she thought. She shrugged innocently. "I read a lot of books about sex. Romance novels can be very explicit, you know."

Jack believed her and smiled. "I'm so glad you like to read," he said.

Rose couldn't deny their relationship to her sorority sisters any longer, because she and Jack were openly affectionate and clearly a couple now. Jack couldn't conceal it from his office staff either. He looked bedraggled every Monday morning after his bedroom marathon with Rose over the weekend and was in a slap happy mood every Friday looking forward to doing it again.

As promised, that spring Savannah Melancon invited Jack and Rose to her very next party at LeBlanc Plantation to celebrate her husband Wayne's fiftieth birthday. The Melancons' twin children, Albert and Amy, were delighted to meet Jack's girlfriend, and the feeling was mutual. Amy's husband Wizard caught Jack alone and said confidentially, "Well done, Handsome Jack."

"Hey, where'd you hear that?" Jack responded.

"I'm the Wizard. I know everything."

Rose and Jack hosted a dinner party at the mansion for Amy and Albert and their spouses a week later. Rose never had a lifelong friend, as she hoped these young couples would become. As Jack said, Amy and Rose were kindred spirits, both of them beautiful, bright and ambitious. They became close friends quickly. BFF's.

CHAPTER 11

Paul Andry received a brief telegram from the monastery in Italy the day of Rose's graduation. He called Jack immediately and read it to him. "She doesn't know me, Jack. You should be the one to give her the news."

"Yes, of course. I'll wait until all of her parties and things are over and she's back home again. I don't want to spoil graduation for her. She's having a great time celebrating."

"When she's feeling up to it, you and Rose need to come over to my office for the reading of the will. He gave me the original to hold for him."

"Sure. I'll call your secretary and set it up later."

After Jack told Rose, he notified Eric's publisher in New York, who made the most of it. It was in all the papers and on all cable news channels. Signed copies of his books became valuable. Tulane's alumni magazine did a full-page article on the three generations of successful and socially prominent Weber men who gave so generously of their time and money to the university and to the city.

Jack took the week off from work and stayed with Rose in her bedroom at the mansion to console her in her grief, dry her tears and spend those precious nights together in each other's arms.

Paul Andry later received a long letter from the monastery and had a clerk from his office deliver it to Rose in person. It was written by a Brother Matthew who spoke English. He reported that Eric had made his confession, received Holy Communion and was given the last rites of the Church. He received comfort care and was at peace with his impending death. He was in a coma for two days. It was his wish to be buried at the monastery. Eric asked that everything he had with him during his stay be sold and donated to the monastery, so there were no personal effects to send back to his home. It more than covered the cost of his stay and expenses. A death certificate written in Italian was sent with the letter.

"I had no idea that Eric was Catholic," Rose said. "He never went to church."

"He was your godfather. He had to be Catholic for that, didn't he?"

Rose laughed nervously to cover the slip-up and slapped her forehead. "Of course. Obviously."

Rose and Jack went together to the lawyer's office two weeks later to open the will. She and Jack had discussed it before. "Do you have any idea what he left you in his will?" Jack asked.

"No, he never mentioned it. It might be the car," she said. "He knew how much I loved it. As for the rest of it, he probably left a big chunk to his college football team. He was a *huge* donor to the Athletic Department. And there were charities he gave to all of his life. Probably left the rest to whatever distant cousins he had. I'm hoping I can stay in the house until it's sold or turned over to an heir. It would give me some time to start a job and find an apartment."

"No need to worry about that," Jack said. "You have money left in your college account. I'll have the rest of the money transferred to your checking account right away. And you can stay with me until you get settled on your own."

Rose smiled at him. "Maybe I will."

When they arrived at Mr. Andry's office for the reading of the will, Jack was immediately struck by the fact that Rose was the only person invited. Rose didn't get the significance of that, but Jack did. He discretely gave Mr. Andry a questioning look, who returned it with a slight nod.

"Jack explained that I'm invited here today because Eric left something for me in his will," she said to Mr. Andry. "He really didn't need to. He did so much for me already."

"Actually, Ms. Alvarez, Eric didn't leave you 'something.' He left you *everything*. The entirety of his estate."

Rose drew in a sharp breath, felt the room spin into darkness, and fainted.

The reading of the will took some time, since it was a long and detailed description of his assets, including a stock portfolio, cash savings, a retirement fund, the cars, his old condo, the house Eric's parents had once owned, the mansion with all of its contents and all rights to his books. Mr. Andry went on and on reading account numbers, legal descriptions of each piece of real estate, contracts for every book deal, even the appraised value of the cars.

Rose absorbed very little of it. Her ears were ringing and she was in shock.

"The old family home and the condo are currently leased to tenants," Mr. Andry explained, "but you will be free to do what you want with them when the leases expire. Of course, you would be well advised to consult a financial planner before disposing of any real estate. You're going to need some tax shelters. You will have to settle up with the IRS also before you sell anything, since the estate is very large and …"

Rose burst out crying and shouted, "Stop! Stop!" She ran out of Andry's office to the elevator, and Jack ran to catch her. He held her in his arms and let her cry. "I can't listen to him anymore, Jack. It sounds so cold. Eric was more than just a bunch of stuff. I want to go home," she sobbed into his chest.

"Sure, Baby, sure we can," he said, holding her head to his chest and rocking her gently. Jack pulled out his cell phone and called Mr. Andry to let him know that they would make an appointment to return later when Rose felt up to it.

Jack took her to a quiet dinner in a little mom-and-pop Italian restaurant in the Lower Garden District neighborhood before they went back to the mansion. She continued to shake her head all through dinner, trying to believe that it was real. "Why? He did so much for me already," she said. The wine helped her to relax and she ate without crying again. "I'm really shocked that he didn't give something to his football team. That was the one great love of his life."

"Maybe it wasn't," Jack said. "You and Eric weren't blood relatives. Was he in love with you?" Jack asked cautiously. "He must have cared for you very much to leave you his entire estate."

Rose shook her head and chuckled. "Eric enjoyed having me around, spoiling me like a pet, showing me the world. But I don't think he ever loved any woman. I didn't realize it at the time, but I think he wanted me to stay with him because I took his mind off the cancer. We had fun together and I guess he was grateful for that."

"Did you love him?"

"Not the way you mean. Eric was my Fairy Godfather, not my Prince Charming."

Jack was relieved to hear it. He had been holding his breath, afraid of her answer.

When they got back to the mansion, (*her* mansion now) Rose stood in the great room and sighed as she gazed around. "I love this place. I don't know what I'm going to do with all this room, but I'll never sell it. Never."

"You won't need to take that job at the convention center now if you don't want to," he said. "You have a home of your own and enough money to last you a lifetime. Instead of working outside, you could work at redecorating the house. Change this dark bachelor pad to suit your own personality. The master suite is yours now. You could make it all pink and ruffle-y and feminine."

"I don't want pink, but I like that idea, Jack," she nodded, giving it some thought. "I'll make the whole house light and airy. I've often thought Eric should put a covered patio across the back of the house with a swing and a barbeque pit and maybe even a swimming pool. I'm a pretty good swimmer now, you know. There's a lot of land back there for whatever."

He took Rose in his arms and kissed her softly. "You have the financial security you needed, a home of your own in your own name and everything you said you had to have before you got married. Will you marry me now, Rose? We could fill up all those bedrooms with kids."

Jack pulled the black velvet ring box out of his pocket, opened it and offered it to her again. Rose smiled up at him and put the ring on her finger. "Yes," she said. "I would love to marry you." Jack stayed the night with her in her old bedroom.

"Before we start planning a wedding, I want to get the house redone. Fresh paint, new drapes, new furniture for the master suite. And I need to settle Eric's estate and pack away all of his papers and personal things. Evelyn wants to retire now, so I asked her to stay long enough to help me hire a replacement and train her."

"I can wait to make it legal," Jack said, "as long as we're together."

CHAPTER 12

The home of Jack Monroe's parents wasn't as grand as her own, but it was a large and beautifully landscaped two-story traditional. Cars lined the long driveway all the way to the street.

"Oh, my goodness!" Rose said nervously. "There's a crowd here! I thought I was going to meet just your parents, Jack."

"Don't be nervous, Baby. It's just immediate family. Mom told them little brother was finally engaged, so they all just invited themselves over to meet you. They're happy for us."

"What if they see that I'm not really like them? Jack is too crazy in love to see or even care, but his family might. Jack says they're all smart. Society people can tell posers from the real thing. Maybe when his passion cools down Jack will see it, too. Or someone from my past will tell him. Oh God! Why didn't I think about this before now?"

After introductions were made all around and the family warmly hugged Rose, Mrs. Monroe ushered everyone into the large family room for cocktails before dinner. Rose was too nervous to drink alcohol and risk letting something slip out, so she asked for a soft drink. They all made casual chit chat while the cook put the finishing touches on the meal.

Mrs. Monroe was elegant and gracious. Despite his successful life, Mr. Monroe still had the manner of a man who had done hard physical labor to get where he was. The eldest son, Kyle, was a college grad who worked with his father since he was a child, and now was mostly in charge of the business. Kyle and his dad were both real estate brokers who bought, renovated and flipped houses. The family also kept a lot of their properties for rentals and leases, making them major landowners in town. Kyle's wife ran the office for them. The second son, Randy, was a CPA and his wife taught school. Jack's only sister, Tonya, was a homemaker. Her husband had his own computer sales and service company.

Rose thought the Monroe's were great people. "I want this kind of family for me and Jack. A happy home, great kids and grandchildren to be proud of. They're all successful, but they act like just regular folks. I want to decorate our house like this one, too. Warm, comfortable, family friendly, great for entertaining but not pretentious."

Over dinner, Rose was reluctant to answer questions about herself, so Jack filled in what she left out. Orphaned at a young age, raised by her grandmother, taken in by her godfather when the grandmother passed away. The family all expressed great sympathy for the tragic losses in her young life.

"The last years living with my godfather were very happy and special for me. He had never married and he enjoyed having me around for company. I think, too, that he felt sorry for me and that's why he wanted to give me the whole world and spoil me rotten," she laughed.

"Jack told us your godfather passed away recently while in Italy. It must be hard to rejoice at your engagement while still grieving for another loss," Mrs. Monroe said sadly.

"Her godfather was my friend and fraternity brother Eric Weber," Jack said, "and he left her his entire estate in his will. I'm marrying Rose for her money," he laughed.

The whole family was in a surprised uproar! *The* Eric Weber? The writer? The one who bought the big Keen mansion on St. Charles Avenue? Holy smokes!

"I met Rose through Eric and fell in love with her instantly," he said reaching for her hand. "I'm surprised she still wants to marry a poor man like me now that she's worth millions."

"You're far from poor and it's not polite to talk about money," she scolded him sweetly. "So change the subject please." He kissed her hand and did as she asked.

"I didn't know Eric Weber," Tonya said, "but I read all of his books because of our brother. Did you know he was *Cade* Monroe before he switched to Jack Monroe? He was our own adventure hero for a while," she laughed.

After dinner, it was nearing sunset and cool enough for them all to adjourn to the sheltered back patio so the smokers could light up. It was still hot enough during the daytime for swimming in the pool, and the grandchildren had left floating toys and flip-flops scattered around from their visit earlier in the day. Landscaping lights in the back yard came on automatically at dark, giving the gardens and trees the look of a magical fairyland.

Eric's back yard wasn't lit up and didn't have a swimming pool, but it would soon enough, Rose assured herself.

"A privileged life of comfort and love," Rose thought with a contented smile. "Our children will have that, too."

Kyle casually asked his father the name of that couple who bought the last house they renovated in Chalmette. "Wasn't it Alvarez?"

Rosalie Alvarez held her breath and froze.

"Yeah, it was Joe Alvarez. Claudette and Joe. Nice folks. Are they kin to you, Rose?" Mr. Monroe asked.

"Not that I know of," she lied with a forced smile. "That's a familiar name in that area, I've been told."

Rose excused herself and went inside to the bathroom. She gulped hands full of water from the faucet and kept telling herself not to cry because her eyes and nose would be red and everyone would notice. She dried her face, took long deep breaths and tried to calm herself.

"I can't go on living a lie. Living in fear of being caught. Joel recognized me at Eric's party and others will, too, eventually. If his family learns the truth, I'll never be welcome here again. Jack would never forgive me for making a fool of him. He would demand a divorce, and rightly so. If we had children by then, they would be devastated to lose their father. I can't marry Jack without telling him the truth first, but he would always know I wasn't his kind. He would live in fear, too, that someone would find out and he would resent me for it. I have to call it off before anyone gets hurt."

Rose waited two weeks before breaking off the engagement and giving Jack his ring on Friday night when he came to pick her up at home. He was devastated. "No, no, Rose. Why? Why would you do this? What changed so fast?"

"It's not you, Jack. I do still love you. It just took me a while to realize that I don't want to marry anybody. I thought I wanted the whole little girl dream of husband and home and children, but when I met your family, I suddenly realized that wasn't the life I wanted at all. I want to be footloose, the way Eric was. Free to come and go and be responsible for nobody but myself."

"I don't believe you," Jack said with tears welling up in his eyes. "You've been alone and lonely too much in your life. I know you're not telling me the truth. Is there someone else?"

"No! Of course not."

"There's something you're holding back. I can see it plainly in your eyes, Rose. What is it? If you're not going to marry me, at least be honest enough to tell me the truth." He held her shoulders to keep her from turning away from him. "Are you wanted by the police?"

"No," she said. "At least I don't think so."

"Have you got a deadly illness?"

"No, I'm fine. And I've had all my shots just like my cats."

"Are you unable to have children? Because I wouldn't care. We can adopt."

"No, it's not that. My doctor says I'm okay and should be able to get pregnant whenever I'm ready."

"Are you a Russian spy?"

"No. I'm not any kind of spy."

"Is there something disturbing you about me?"

"No, Jack. You are so wonderful. If I were going to marry anyone, I couldn't find anyone better," she said.

"THEN WHY?" he shouted angrily.

"I … I can't talk anymore. I'm sorry for hurting you, Jack," she said looking at the floor, with tears running down her cheeks. "Please go."

"I'll go for now," he said softly, "but I won't give up." He kissed her and left.

Rose wouldn't take Jack's phone calls, and she wouldn't answer the door when he came by.

CHAPTER 13

Cal Westerman frowned as soon as he and Jack walked into the steakhouse. "Oh, hell! He spotted me. I'll have to go over and say hello," he said. "The guy's a sleazebag, but he's a paying client."

"That's what you get for being a criminal defense attorney, Cal. You get low life clients," laughed Jack. "Go make nice and I'll wait in the bar. Don't take too long, though. I'm starved."

The client, Sam "The Slam" Montet, got his nickname for being a sadistic bastard who slammed women around for fun. He was a deputy with the Plaquemines Parish Sheriff's Office, so as long he had his fun close to home, the working girls didn't file any complaints. Wouldn't do any good anyway. The parish sheriff was Sammy's brother and the parish president was a cousin.

The only time Sammy needed a criminal defense attorney was when he got into trouble in New Orleans when he came to party. He picked up young prostitutes in the Quarter and gave them a tough going over, including bruises, black eyes and cut lips, but working girls in the city didn't report him to NOPD either. Being slapped around was just one of the hazards of the profession.

It was the women higher up on the social scale who accused him of assault. Sam Montet was a good-looking man. He dressed well when he came to town and he could be very charming when he met a new lady. A night of dining and dancing with a handsome and witty new guy was thrilling for a lot of single young women. If they didn't invite him in for sex at the end of the night, Sammy beat them up. It wasn't as much fun as sex, but he enjoyed it anyway. He had been arrested many times, but Sammy's grandparents had money and always came up with enough of it to pay off his victims to drop the charges and pay the attorney fees to Cal.

Sammy was dining with a beautiful young lady when Cal came over to their table. "Where y'at, Sammy?" Cal said jovially and shook Sammy's hand.

"How's the legal business these days, Mr. Westerman?" Sammy asked.

"Not so good when you behave yourself," Cal teased with a laugh.

"Go on, Cal, you're going to give my lovely date the wrong idea about me. This clown is my lawyer, Cal Westerman." he said to Rose with a charming smile. "Cal, this is Miss Rose Alvarez."

"A pleasure, Miss Alvarez," Cal said. "I've got a friend waiting for me in the bar. You two have a good evening and enjoy your meal."

The food hadn't arrived yet, so Rose excused herself to go to the ladies room. She didn't see Cal and Jack in the bar when she went by, but they saw her.

Jack's mouth fell open. "Don't let your tongue hang out, Jack. That classy doll is here with my sleazebag client," Cal told him. "Can you believe it? I sure would hate to see a face like that get busted up."

"Cal, that's my ex-fiancée, Rose! I've got to get her away from that creep before she gets hurt!"

"Let me take care of it, Jack. When I get Sammy to leave the restaurant, you go in and sit with your girl. Have dinner and take her home in your car. Maybe you two can patch things up."

"How are you going to get him to leave and not take Rose with him?"

Cal explained his plan and Jack liked it. They shook hands and Cal went back to Sammy's table.

"Sam, my friend and I have a problem and we need your help. Would you please come and talk with us in the bar for a minute. This is big and *urgent*!" Cal pulled Sam away from the table and rushed him to meet Jack.

"My friend Jack here recognized your date."

"Mr. Montet, I hate to tell you this," Jack said confidentially, "but that hot little number with you tonight is the governor's mistress! The governor and I are good friends, so I know her. He went to Ms. Alvarez's house tonight to see her and now he's got State Troopers out looking for her. You can't take her home. The gov is there waiting for her."

"You've got to get out of here quick, Sammy," Cal said.

"But I can't just walk out on my date," Sammy protested. "What will she think? She's a very classy uptown lady. We haven't eaten yet!"

"Don't worry," Jack said. "I'll explain everything to her, we'll have a nice dinner and I'll drive her home. I'll tell the governor that I spotted her with a girlfriend at the bar and she wanted to go right home when I told her he was looking for her. He knows me and trusts me. It'll be fine, I promise. But you need to go *now*!"

Sam Montet peeled off a couple of big bills from his money clip and shoved them into Jack's hand as Cal was pushing him toward the door. "Take care of the tab, Jack, and thanks."

Jack and Cal stared straight-faced at the exit door for a few beats, then cracked up laughing. "Go take care of your fiancée," Cal said with a pat on Jack's back. "I'm going home."

Rose was startled when Jack came over and sat in Sam's chair. "What are you doing? Where's Sam Montet? Is he all right? Did you do something to him, Jack?"

"No. I told him that I was crazy in love with you and I was trying to get us back together again. Being a decent and sympathetic gentleman, he left and wished me good luck." He refilled Rose's glass of wine and poured one for himself. "You look so beautiful tonight. I've missed you. By the way, I read recently that you made a large donation to the homeless shelter for teens in Eric's name. And my friend Albert Melancon tells me he has seen you about town at various charity events. I'm glad to see you're doing well."

Before Rose could speak, the waiter brought the sizzling steaks and baked potatoes that Sammy had ordered when they arrived. Jack ate Sammy's steak, medium rare, just the way he liked it. They finished eating with little to say, and Jack took her home.

"Jack, you have to let it go. You have to stop calling and banging on my door."

"I'll stop pushing on one condition. Tell me the truth about why you won't marry me. I have to know or I'll never have any peace."

"Alright," she said sadly. "Come over tomorrow after work and I'll tell you everything." She held up her right hand. "The truth, the whole truth and nothing but the truth, so help me God." Well, not exactly the *whole* truth, she admitted to herself. Some of the intimate details would hurt him too much.

The following night, Evelyn escorted Jack to the front parlor where Rose was waiting for him. "I'll bring in a fresh pot of coffee," she said to Rose, and returned with a tray quickly. She poured two cups, then left and closed the door so they could have privacy. Returning to her kitchen, Evelyn crossed herself and silently prayed that Jack and Rose would work out their problems, whatever they were, and get married.

Rose didn't look like a college girl any more. She had become the "classy uptown lady" like Sam Montet said. She was the queen of her castle.

"Before I start," Rose said, "I want you to promise me two things. First, that you will not say anything until I'm finished. No arguments, interruptions, comments, questions or anything else."

Jack nodded and made a gesture that he was zipping his mouth shut.

"Second, I want you to swear that you will never repeat any of this to anyone. I hope to make my way in this town with a decent reputation."

Jack crossed his heart in silence and nodded his agreement.

"When I went through Eric's personal papers, I found that he kept spiral notebooks that were sort of a journal, but with all kinds of other notes as well. A hodge-podge of story ideas, phone logs, business discussions, his medical treatments, things his psychiatrist told him, his daily thoughts and activities. There were boxes of these notebooks going back for years, so what I'm going to tell you includes some of his secrets, too. Do you swear to keep his information private also?"

Jack nodded.

"You'll probably hate me forever, but at least be grateful that I didn't marry you and ruin your life." Rose summoned up her courage and began.

"Almost everything you know about me is a lie and I couldn't base our marriage on that. You deserve better. At the same time, I was too ashamed to tell you the truth. I'll start at the beginning, with the truth about my parents."

Jack listened in stunned silence.

CHAPTER 14

Rose was shaking as she told her story. "My parents were minimum wage people who dropped out of high school because of an accidental pregnancy and blamed each other for all their miseries. They regularly got drunk on payday, when there was a payday, and bashed each other around. The New Orleans Police Department came to break up screaming, cursing fights between them and occasionally taking my father to jail for disturbing the peace. There never was any money to bail him out, which wasn't all that bad for any of us. He was fed three good meals every day, my mother had some rest while he served his time and I didn't have to leave the house to avoid getting caught in the middle. I wasn't usually their target unless I got in the way."

It was painful for Rose to remember when her days were filled with fear and shame, and the intense loneliness of being an only child, unwanted and unloved. Mostly, they ignored her like she wasn't there. Babies frequently waste away and die if they're simply fed and diapered but rarely cuddled, like they do in orphanages in some third-world countries. But Rose didn't die. She eventually stopped crying for mother because mother never came to the crib except to do what was required.

Rose's parents had no idea that they won the genetic lottery with their only child, who was both bright and beautiful, and had all the gifts for a stellar future. Rosalie learned to walk and talk very early. She also learned very early when to be quiet and disappear.

Mrs. Alvarez was a cold woman, more of a caretaker than a mother to Rose. She cooked the meals and did the laundry, but she never once told Rose that she loved her or showed any sign of affection. The only time she talked to Rose was to complain about something. The closest thing Rose had for a mother figure was Grandma Alvarez.

Grandma didn't get along with Rosalie's mother and wasn't welcome at their house, even to visit her only grandchild. She was allowed to send gifts, mostly clothes and books, and talk to the child on the phone. Rosalie loved books and learned to read and write before she started first grade. Grandma recognized that the child was gifted early on, and desperately prayed that she would rise above her circumstances.

Rose wasn't just bright, she was also emotionally strong. Grandma often told her, "You're made of steel, Rose. Nothing is gonna break you. Use your brains to get an education and you'll have a good life. Be a good girl and trust God."

Grandma Alvarez lived within a block of the local Catholic school. She persuaded them to take Rosalie on partial scholarship and paid the rest of the tuition from her little pension. She sacrificed everything she had.

Rosalie loved to learn, but what she loved most about going to school was she got to see her grandmother regularly. Grandma walked over to every school function and sometimes brought sandwiches so she and Rosalie could eat lunch together on the playground. Grandma Alvarez was a warm and loving person, who made Rosalie feel that she was worthy of being loved. The second thing Rosalie loved about school was that it was a long way from her neighborhood, and nobody at school knew her parents or anything about her home life. She never felt ashamed at school.

The public library close to Rosalie's home was a clean, quiet, safe place to escape from her miserable home life when she wasn't in school. Rosalie's mind was like a sponge and she was interested in everything. For hours in the library, she did homework and read. By second grade, she was beyond children's books. By sixth grade, she was reading classic literature, current fiction, history, magazines, newspapers, pop culture and *The Art of the Deal.*

Grandma Alvarez died of natural causes, peacefully in her sleep, when Rosalie was in eighth grade. It was a triple tragedy for the child. First, she had to transfer to the failing and often violent public school in her neighborhood, where even the limited classes for gifted children were lagging far behind the opportunities available in the private schools. Second, she had to leave behind the best friends she grew up with from first grade. Finally, and worst of all, she lost the only family member she truly loved and who loved her back.

Rosalie had no one to comfort her in her grief, but she did what her grandmother wanted her to do. She stayed strong and trusted God.

Rosalie spent most of every summer in the library or hanging out on the street with kids her age in the neighborhood. Anything to stay away from home. Even if she stayed away from dawn to dark, her mother never came looking for her.

Rosalie wasn't in the house the day her mother stabbed and mortally wounded her father with a kitchen knife in a drunken brawl. Her father pulled a gun, and shot and killed Rosalie's mother before he bled to death on the kitchen floor. Rosalie went into the house when she heard the gunshot, finding the horrifying sight and blood all over the kitchen floor. A neighbor called 911. Rosalie screamed and tried to run outside to get away from the dead bodies, but her bare feet slipped in the blood on the linoleum floor and she landed on her back. Too shocked to move again, she stayed on the kitchen floor, wiped her bloody hands on her shirt and closed her eyes tight until the police came. She was still trembling when a female officer took her to the bathroom to clean her up and help her change clothes before taking her away.

"I was in shock, unable to talk for a long time. I remember being taken to the police station while they decided what to do with me. I was fourteen and terrified. I thought they were going to put me in jail because I was to blame. It would have been better for me if they had. But they sent me to relatives that night. People I didn't know."

Rosalie was still grieving for her grandmother, but didn't grieve much for her parents. It wasn't like they had that kind of relationship. She hardly knew them, really. They were just a couple of people who lived in the same house with her and bought the groceries. Rosalie had been a *de facto* orphan and her own caretaker for years.

"I was sent to live with my Aunt Claudette and Uncle Joe Alvarez in Chalmette. They were churchgoing people who had good jobs and a nice home. They didn't associate with the trashy Alvarez side of the family. Their children were already grown and gone, and Aunt Claudette didn't want to take in another child. However, Uncle Joe said they had to because it was their Christian duty. I didn't expect them to love me, since even my own parents didn't, but thought if I helped with the housework and kept quiet and out of the way, Aunt Claudette would accept me in time. I had been told by neighbors that the high school in Chalmette was pretty good, so I looked forward to starting in the fall and making new friends again. But I didn't get the chance."

Rose's voice cracked with emotion. She took a sip of coffee and rattled the cup when she put it down. Her hands were shaking. "This is still hard to talk about even after all this time."

Uncle Joe crawled into bed with her one night and took her by force. His face was rough and hairy and he smelled like a wet dog. Rosalie wept from fear and pain, but didn't cry out because he threatened to kill her if she did. He grunted and pawed at her roughly like an animal, his rough hands making her skin hurt.

After he pulled his pants on and went back to his own bed, Rosalie went to the bathroom to wash herself and try to get rid of the stink of him, but the smell stayed in her nose and her mind. Every time a man touched her after that, the smell of Uncle Joe came back to her. She had bruises on her arms, legs and shoulders. She hurt all over.

She staggered from the bathroom in a daze, traumatized again, trying to stuff down all the feelings of grief, shame, hopelessness and fear. She pulled the bedspread off the bed and wrapped it around her nakedness as she sat down on the floor trembling and crying. The only answer was to run away and hide. She got dressed and packed a change of clothes in her black vinyl tote bag, accidently stepping on Uncle Joe's wallet near her bed. Joe hadn't noticed it missing in his rush to pull on his pants and leave the room. She took his sixty-three dollars in cash and tossed the wallet under the bed, hoping that Aunt Claudette would find it when she cleaned the floor and kill her husband for what he'd done. But she needn't have bothered.

Claudette already knew that her husband was a bastard who was inordinately friendly with young girls in the neighborhood. When Joe asked where the girl was the next day, his wife just said that she ran away. They both knew why and never discussed it again. Aunt Claudette didn't report the girl missing, because she didn't want her back.

As she left the house and walked away in the dark, Rosalie held her head up and straightened her shoulders. She remembered her grandmother's words to her. "I will stay strong, Grandma, like you said. But, I'm sorry, I don't trust God anymore." She had taken a small paring knife from Aunt Claudette's kitchen and carried it inside the pocket of her jeans.

"I was ready to commit murder that night," she said to Jack. "I imagined myself stabbing any man who tried to touch me. That little kitchen knife stayed within reach all the time. It helped me to feel safe and in control, like I was some badass gang member."

She thumbed a ride from Chalmette to downtown New Orleans and walked until she found the Café du Monde, where late-night party people in fancy clothes were sobering up with coffee at the outdoor tables before trying to drive home. She had coffee and beignets, the square doughnuts covered with powdered sugar, and finished as dawn started to light the sky with red streaks. She thought of something she read in a book. "Red sky at night, sailor's delight. Red sky at morning, sailor take warning." Looking at the sky, she nodded and said to herself, *Take warning. Damned right. They better take warning of me.*

Jack had tears in his eyes and held his hands over his mouth to keep from saying anything until he recovered his composure. He pulled a handkerchief out of his pocket, dabbed his eyes and blew his nose, then signaled for Rose to continue.

"While I was at Tulane, I found out about a support group for rape survivors and I attended every week for a year. It helped a lot."

CHAPTER 15

I stayed at a homeless shelter for teens for a couple of days, but the people who ran the place asked too many questions and enforced too many rules. They were going to call Child Protection and have me put in a foster home, so I split. I couldn't trust any adult, so I wouldn't live in a shelter or foster home or anywhere else where other people had the control and could do what they wanted to me."

She had been abused, neglected and molested by the people who should have loved and cared for her. She was angry, lonely and scared, but fiercely determined to survive, no matter what it took. Living on the streets was like being in a jungle. Hell, living with other people was like being in a jungle, too. She had to be vigilant all the time. Rosalie shut off her feelings and became tough real fast.

Like many rape victims, Rosalie turned the tables on men and used them the way she had been used. She used sex to take what she wanted and take some revenge when she could.

It was easy for a willing homeless girl to find a warm bed in a hotel room or apartment, especially a girl who had the face and body of a porn star like Rosalie. Naturally, she preferred to sleep alone. Sex was just a damned nuisance and not something she ever considered engaging in for pleasure. No man ever tried to please her. Even if they had, she couldn't forget the feel and smell of Uncle Joe.

But sex got her food and shelter without resorting to dealing drugs on the street, and it was legal. She would never accept cash money from a man, because that was prostitution and illegal; and in spite of her way of life, she never considered herself a hooker. She was just a survivor.

"I lived on the streets for two years. The only friends I had were other homeless teenagers like me, until the day I struck up a conversation with a middle-aged gay couple, Steven and Gary, at the Café Du Monde. They lived and worked in the French Quarter. I liked them right away and they liked me. We became friends. They knew I was homeless, so they treated me to a meal or gave me a few bucks whenever we met. It was good to have friends who were kind and didn't expect sex in return."

Steven was a fashion buyer for a major department store. Rose told him that men sometimes took her shopping and bought her clothes, and she wanted to be able to pick out the good stuff. She asked Steven to teach her what to look for. So Steven took Rose under his wing, taught her a few things about clothes and was constantly entertained by her quick wit and her stories of life on the street.

The truth was, men didn't buy clothes for her. She stole them. She just wanted to be sure that she was picking up the good stuff, not cheap knock-offs. But she couldn't tell Steven that.

With her high quality little wardrobe, Rose didn't look unkept or homeless. Wherever she went, she looked like the respectable people who belonged there. She stashed her extra clothes and shoes in the storage room of the little laundromat where she washed her clothes, and brought the female owner whatever pretty little items she picked up from time to time.

Rosalie still found refuge many days in the public library. But there were other interesting and educational places that provided free shelter from the weather, like book stores, courtrooms, art galleries, St. Louis Cathedral, and big hotel lobbies.

She sometimes got in to free lectures for convention people at some big hotel and helped herself to the pastries and coffee set up at the back of the room. If she was caught without a proper registration badge, she would act surprised and rush off to the ladies room "where it probably fell off earlier." Sometimes she picked up someone else's badge at registration. Whatever worked.

Every now and then, she would flirt with one of the male conventioneers and get invited to an expensive lunch, making the guy practically bug-eyed at the belief that he would get lucky with this hot little number. After lunch, she would make some excuse to leave with his hotel room key and promise to meet him in an hour. Of course, she never did. If the guy was really nice and gentlemanly over lunch, she felt a little sorry for tricking him. Mostly, though, she just felt contempt for men and enjoyed her little victories.

No matter where she spent her days, she learned something, got a free meal, or at least escaped the heat on the street. That all worked fine for daytime, but "house sitting" was her first choice for a place to spend the night.

CHAPTER 16

Rosalie Alvarez had the B&E skills of a cat burglar and could get into just about any empty house without making a sound, setting off an alarm or leaving a trace that she was ever there.

She learned how to do it from her friend Sonny, one of the other teens staying at the homeless shelter in the French Quarter. Sonny called it "house sitting." He had been doing it for a long time and never got caught. The only time he went back to the shelter was when it was too cold to stay in an empty house with no utilities turned on, or to stay with his buddies at the empty warehouse down by the river.

Sonny taught her all of the critical rules for house sitting without getting caught. Most importantly, never turn on a light or any appliance that would make a sound and attract the attention of neighbors. Never open a curtain. Use a tiny keychain flashlight to get around the house and locate necessities after dark. Eat what's in the fridge, but never cook anything. Eat in the kitchen where it's easy to clean up messes. Sleep in any room except the master suite, because the homeowner might notice if the bed is made up differently. Stay only one night. Take only one good item of clothing if things fit you, or one inexpensive accessory. The lady of the house will think she misplaced it, not that a burglar left the jewelry box in plain sight and took a blouse. Make a couple of sandwiches for the road. Before you go, clean away every trace that you were ever there. Wash and put away dishes. Put your wet bath towel in the trash and take all trash with you when you leave. Don't give the homeowner any reason to suspect a break-in and call the cops, because sooner or later, they will catch you.

The best time for house sitting was the summer. Families go on vacation or relocate while the kids are out of school. The second best time was Thanksgiving week when people leave town to visit grandma. Lots of nice places to pick from, and there was always food in the house somewhere.

"Of the many houses I broke into, the one I liked best was this very house that I now own," she told Jack. "Funny, isn't it? It was called the Keen Mansion back then, before Eric bought it. In this place, I could dream big and feel almost rich for a little while. I spent the night here a dozen times before Eric bought it. It was priced in the millions, so it took a few years to find a buyer. Even when it was empty, the utilities stayed on for realtors to show the property, so it was warm in winter, cool in summer and all the conveniences worked."

"I was in awe of the place. I thought the light grey stone walls and tall windows all around made it look like a castle."

It was built high off the ground with massive stone stairs leading up to the wide porch across the front. The second-story balcony with shiny black wrought iron railings was held up over the porch by stout columns.

With nine bedrooms, six bathrooms and extensive flowering gardens, it took up most of the block on St. Charles Avenue. A brick driveway led through the wrought iron fence to the back garage, with brick walking paths continuing through the gardens to fountains and oak trees. Every tree was surrounded by lush greenery like a living tutu with ferns, peace lilies and the broad shiny leaves of the aspidistra plants.

The mansion had a spacious bedroom and bath just off the kitchen for the housekeeper. Those rooms had no windows, so Rosalie could close the door and turn on the lights in there day or night to read, eat, bathe or whatever. It was a sweet little set-up.

Eric moved in a week before Thanksgiving and there was no sign of a housekeeper or any other people living there with him. Since he lived alone, Rosalie hoped he would be leaving to visit family for the holidays so she could stay there again. Rose did her usual surveillance to check it out.

On Monday, Eric left in a taxi rather than his big Humvee. He took a carry-on bag with him, a sure sign that he was flying somewhere and would be gone at least overnight, maybe longer. Rosalie was overjoyed! She waited until dark and slipped into the house her usual way.

Once inside the mansion, Rosalie went straight to the kitchen for food. An occupied house always had food of some kind, and Rose wasn't particular.

A wall calendar in the kitchen had a line drawn through all of Thanksgiving week, with the notation "BELIZE" on it. Rosalie was so excited she nearly shouted. She danced a little jig and repeated softly over and over, "A week! A whole week! You go to your paradise, Mr. Rich Man, and I will stay here in mine!" It would be safe to stay for more than one night when you knew for sure the owner wasn't coming back.

She continued singing softly to herself while she checked out the fridge. As Sonny taught her, she unscrewed the light inside so it couldn't shine a light out the window every time she opened the door, and used her tiny keychain flashlight to find what she wanted inside. The commercial-sized fridge and freezer were well stocked.

The owner had a small party before flying off to Belize, and there were plenty of leftovers in the fridge and pantry. A tray with meats and cheeses. Chips and fancy crackers for dips. Wine, beer and soft drinks. A half-empty bakery box of little cakes and pastries, with the delivery ticket still on it. "Eric Weber" the ticket said. She recognized the name. His books were in the public library and prominently displayed in book stores.

"Thank you, Mr. Weber for leaving me a feast!" Rosalie whispered happily to herself. In most houses where the occupant expected to be gone for a while, the best she could hope for was leftovers, breakfast cereal and stale cookies. This guy had left her plenty of the good stuff. She carried food into the housekeeper's room, put everything on the bed, closed the door and turned on the light.

She opened a bottle of red wine, for starters. She couldn't pronounce the name, but in a house like this, it had to be something expensive. "Tasty," she said with a low growl. Sipping it slowly from the bottle, she soaked her cares away in the maid's deep bathtub. She put on a giant t-shirt she got from the owner's closet and wore it as a nightshirt. After eating her fill of the party foods, she went to sleep in the housekeeper's room, feeling very lucky.

The next day, Tuesday, she started exploring each room in the house thoroughly, taking her time, since she was going to be there for several days. The house was sold with all the existing furniture, mostly large antique pieces. Rose recognized it from when she stayed in the house in the past.

The great room was huge and all of the rooms downstairs opened into it except the kitchen. There was a grand piano, beautifully upholstered sofas and chairs clustered in conversation groups, lots of little tables and lamps and a couple of matching oriental rugs in rich colors covering the marble floor. The upholsteries, decorative accessories and wall color picked up the colors of the greens, blues and creams from the rugs. A five tiered crystal chandelier hung in the center of the room.

Rose had never seen the room with the lights on, but guessed that it must be beautiful.

The smoking room with the pool table had dark paneling on the walls, dark wood floors and big leather chairs around the fireplace. A stuffed deer head with a gigantic rack of antlers hung over the fireplace. *"His man cave,"* she thought to herself. Photographs and souvenirs around the room were from his adventures mountain climbing, white water rafting, scuba diving, hunting, skiing, sailing and deep sea fishing. Mr. Weber had his college football jersey and a pennant framed and hanging on the wall.

She challenged the absent Mr. Weber to a game of pool. "So, football hero, you really suck at pool, I see," she laughed when she sank a good shot. "I win. You owe me a hundred bucks." She played pool for hours in semi-darkness, then found a deck of cards at a poker table in the corner of the room near a window and played solitaire until the daylight no longer filtered through the slit in the curtains. There was still some light coming into the kitchen, so she brought the cards in there to continue her game.

The kitchen was big enough to service a major restaurant, with every kind of appliance and utensil you could think of. Some people lived in apartments smaller than that kitchen. The china and crystal were elegant and fancy, like this was the White House or something. She imagined they looked like jewelry in a store window when the table was set. Everything glittering silver and gold. The butler's pantry had even more stuff, including locked cabinets for the silver serving pieces. Glass front cabinets held the formal china, crystal stemware and typical "party pieces" like big punch bowls and platters. There was a wine cooler, a little desk area for the cook or housekeeper and open shelves for cookbooks and assorted little baskets for storage. One cabinet held table linens.

Rose frowned at the beautiful array of things displayed before her. "All this stuff just for rich people to entertain other rich people."

A complete gym at the back of the house was filled with all kinds of equipment, machines and weights. "Eric, do you like to keep buff, like you're still the football hero?" She answered for him in a very deep voice. "Why, yes, Rosalie, I'm still a macho, macho man." She strutted around the room humming the song to herself.

The next room that interested her was the owner's library and office. Heavy drapes covered the windows, so she used her tiny flashlight to check it out. He used the big old antique desk that came with the house. The walls were lined with book shelves floor to ceiling. He displayed football trophies, college souvenirs and writing awards among the books. Some of the books were left over from the previous owner. Mr. Weber added his own treasures, including the books he wrote himself. Nineteen best sellers so far, but Rosalie didn't like any of them. Macho adventure stories weren't her thing. "Former jock writes big books in his old age for semiliterate people and makes a shit pile of money. Is this a great country, or what?" She sat in his executive desk chair and read the mail on his desk, making sure to put everything back exactly as she found it. Invitations, business mail, newsletter from his old fraternity.

Eric Weber had a primo sound system in his office, with a collection of music to die for. "Does relaxing with your music help you to write so beautifully, Mr. Weber?" she asked in a chirpy flirtatious voice.

"Why, yes, Rosalie," she answered for him again, sounding very imperial. "I'm currently working on the Great American Novel."

"How kind of you to grant me an interview for People Magazine," she said as she sashayed around the room. "May I try out your big cushy arm chair and your headphones? How delicious life is for you!"

The chair was meant for a person who was big and tall, and it swallowed her up. She chuckled remembering a line from Eliza Doolittle's song, and sang it softly to herself. "All I want is a room somewhere, far away from the cold night air, and one enormous chair." She sighed contentedly and agreed with Eliza, that it was indeed "loverly."

She put the headphones on and listened to the selection that Eric listened to last time. It was a piece by Chopin. She liked to listen to classical music at a local used books and records shop on Magazine Street, where the owner taught her music appreciation from Beethoven to the Beatles.

"Chopin! Good choice, Eric. You're not a complete Philistine." She took a book of Louisiana history from the shelf and brought it to the maid's bedroom to read before going to sleep. Louisiana history was taught in high school, but since she never got there, she taught it to herself as best she could.

The third day, Wednesday, she explored the master bedroom and bath upstairs, opening every drawer and closet. The bathroom had a skylight, making it easy for her to check out everything without needing her flashlight during the day. The bathroom floor was a beautiful black marble, there was a big soaker tub with a small chandelier above it, and a glass-enclosed shower big enough for four people at once. The bath towels were supersized, sweet-smelling and plush. The bath soap smelled expensive, too. She took a fresh bar, still wrapped in pretty paper, from a storage cabinet and saved it for the laundromat owner.

The medicine cabinet had the usual things, no interesting drugs or medications. "Well, Eric, you're either very healthy for an old dude, or you don't care enough to go to a doctor."

There were no condoms in the bedside table or bathroom. "Odd. Why is that, Eric? Don't care about safe sex? Did your joy stick quit working? No, probably not, or you would have Viagra around here somewhere. Or could you be gay, *Mr. Macho Man?"*

Eric left two folded fifty dollar bills in a pair of jeans hanging on a hook in his closet. "You owe me a hundred bucks for losing the game of pool, so I'll take these," she said and slipped out of the house after dark. A rich guy wouldn't even remember that he left a little pocket money in his jeans. At first, she thought about how many meals that hundred bucks could buy. But like a kid alone in a candy store, she wanted a once-in-a-lifetime treat that might never come along again. She wanted a foolish luxury. Something beautiful and expensive.

The St. Charles Avenue streetcar was a pretty nice ride, rocking gently and clacking with a soothing rhythm along the tracks. It passed along magnificent old mansions lining both sides of the street and under a canopy of ancient oak trees. Most of the giant houses were already decorated outside and lit up for Christmas. Hedges and wrought iron fences were strung with lights and garlands, a holly wreath hung from every front door, poinsettias in big pots were clustered on porches and steps. The decorated houses looked like they were ready for great holiday parties and for happy families to celebrate together, but it made Rose feel lonely. Always an outsider looking in. She shook her head to dispel the thought and told herself to get over it.

The streetcar took her to a little lingerie boutique on the avenue that stayed open late from Thanksgiving week to Christmas. She bought herself an expensive Christmas present there with Mr. Weber's money, a black silk teddy, like one she saw in a fashion magazine once. Then she rode the streetcar to Fat Harry's to get a shrimp po-boy and a draft beer on the way back. A pleasant night out boosted her spirits.

Sonny, her friend from the homeless shelter, spotted her when she got off the streetcar. Sonny was sixteen and had been living on the street for a couple of years. He had been a smoker for as long as he could remember. He had ink pen tattoos on his arms and hands and he wore black fingernail polish. Sonny was skinny and pale, like most of the boys he hung out with in the Quarter. They panhandled, sold drugs and shoplifted to get cash, which was spent mostly on cigarettes, beer and grass.

"Where y'at, Rosie Girl?" he greeted her happily with a hug. "Ain't seen ya' around for a while. Where ya' been stayin'?" he asked.

"House sittin' here and there," she said nonchalantly.

"You must be doin' good on the rich side of town. You pick up a sugar daddy?" he asked, pointing to the pretty little pink tote bag she got at the lingerie shop.

"No, just picked up his money while he was out of town," she laughed. "Gotta little bit left. Come in with me and I'll buy you a burger and a beer." Rose took a driver's license from a previous house sitting so she could get into bars and pass herself off as twenty-one.

Fat Harry's was a popular college hangout where the atmosphere was happy all the time, but especially the day before Thanksgiving when everybody was in a party mood and ready for the long weekend. In spite of the cold night, the sidewalk tables were full, so Rose and Sonny went inside and eventually grabbed a spot when other customers were leaving.

Rose was happy to be able to eat and talk and laugh with a friend that night, but Sonny didn't stay long in the bar after he ate. A college hangout wasn't his kind of place. He was more at home in some nasty little dive north of the Quarter with old drunks and whores. "It was good catchin' up with ya' but I gotta go, Rosie, and catch the streetcar back to the Quarter. I'm meetin' a new customer down on Rampart Street in a while, and Dago's not the kind you want to keep waitin,' ya' know?"

"Still dealin' *dama blanca*?"

"Yeah, Girl, you gotta do whatcha gotta do to make it on the street, ya' know?"

"Yeah. Me, too. Be careful, okay?" They hugged goodbye. Rosalie stayed a while longer and enjoyed the beer and the music.

On the streetcar ride back to the mansion, Rosalie thought wistfully to herself, "Regular people do this all the time, like it's nothing. Take a streetcar or a cab, go where they want, buy what they like, meet up with their friends. Well tonight, I'm regular people."

Once back at the house, she took a shower, washed her hair, put on her silk teddy and admired herself in the mirror. She danced around seductively, tossing her long thick hair, singing softly and shaking her stuff like a rock star.

The only nice clothes Rosalie had with her were two outfits she took while house sitting. They replaced the used clothes she got from the homeless shelter. Everything she carried with her fit into her large black tote bag that also served as her purse. The silk teddy let her feel rich for a while. The lady of a fine house like this would have plenty of pretty things, like expensive lacey lingerie. There weren't any women's clothes in the house, but she might find something else useful before she left.

She took a glass of the red wine to Mr. Weber's office to listen to music with the headphones so she could play it as loud as she wanted without making a sound. She took a lap blanket with her from a sofa in the family room and settled comfortably into the big cushy armchair. In the dark room slowly sipping wine, she fell asleep full and happy.

"I didn't hear Eric when he came home about ten o'clock, cutting his trip short by three days."

CHAPTER 17

Eric had been seeing Dr. Cushman for years because of persistent depression. He used rigorous daily exercise to increase endorphins rather than taking drugs, but sometimes it just wasn't enough. From the beginning, Dr. Cushman was concerned about suicide.

A year before Eric bought the mansion, Cushman asked him, "Do you still keep the .38 in your desk?"

Eric nodded.

"When was the last time you put it to your head?"

"Yesterday," he answered calmly. "I couldn't think of any reason to keep going. What's the point of writing books and making more money? It won't change anything. This time bomb in my brain is still ticking. Then Evelyn yelled from the kitchen because the faucet broke and water was squirting everywhere. I went in and fixed it for her. I thought, maybe that's a reason to keep on living. My housekeeper needs me." Eric laughed at himself.

"Eric," Dr. Cushman said, "I asked you to unload the gun and put the bullets somewhere else in your apartment. In a locked drawer. In the time it takes you to get the bullet and go back to your desk, you might find another reason to live. Have you done that yet?"

"No, not yet. I'm … thinking about it," he answered with a shrug.

When Eric moved into the mansion, he did as his psychiatrist suggested and locked the bullets in the silver storage cabinet in the pantry. He was on an emotional high, thinking of all the great big parties he could have in his big new house and didn't expect he would want the bullets again.

But the thoughts of suicide crashed in on him again, unexpectedly, when he came home from Belize.

Eric left his coat and carry-on bag by the door and went to the kitchen first to pour himself a stiff drink. Then he intended to unlock the silver cabinet in the butler's pantry and take out the box of bullets.

Eric was aggravated that his trip to Belize was a waste of time and money. The guys he was meeting were old friends who went scuba diving with him before, but on this trip they brought along two of the most obnoxious bimbos this side of Miami. They were whiney, demanding bitches who found some-thing to complain about all day long. The guys didn't seem to mind having the girls around because they had big boobs and liked sex, but Eric couldn't wait to get home.

The depression hit him like a rock. He felt very alone. Why not eat the bullet?

When he turned on the kitchen lights, his mouth fell open in shock.

Dirty dishes and coffee cups in the sink. An open bottle of wine on the counter. A nearly empty box of pastries and little cakes. A half-completed game of solitaire spread out on the breakfast table. How did someone get in the house and not trigger the alarm? The intruder must be gone now. There was no sound from anywhere and all the rooms were dark.

He slowly and quietly went from room to room, turning on lights and looking for evidence of damage or theft. That would be the first thing the police would want to know. Was anything missing? He didn't touch anything, in case the burglar left fingerprints.

When he opened his office door, the light shining in from the great room revealed an incredibly beautiful woman sleeping in his big arm chair. She had nothing on but a thin black silk teddy that left nothing to the imagination. Her lap blanket had slipped off and was in a heap on the floor in front of her.

"Holy shit!" He mouthed the words silently. He stood in the door for a while, savoring the sight of her, wishing that she had fallen asleep in his bed instead of in his office. *"Maybe she will later,"* he thought, smiling to himself.

Eric loved beautiful women, but he didn't particularly like them. He found them boring or manipulative, except as partners in bed. He met great women now and then that he really enjoyed being with, but they were always married, or old or off having their own adventurous lives. Or they were looking for a rich husband.

Eric was comfortable in the company of men, because they understood and respected each other. He treated every man as an equal and never acted self-important with them. Men liked Eric. He was a man's man. Big, masculine and athletic. Women liked him for the same reasons.

Although they flocked to him, Eric didn't enjoy the company of women. He couldn't figure out what they were thinking, what they wanted or why they sometimes got mad at him for no apparent reason. They were unpredictable. He lived his life in a man's world and women were aliens. He enjoyed superficial short-term relationships among the aliens, because he was very good at getting them to his bed. But they weren't people to Eric. They were objects of physical pleasure. They were lovely to look at, like great works of art. They smelled like exotic intoxicating flowers. A woman's skin felt like cream on his lips and long silky hair was the most luxurious thing he ever touched. Women delighted all of his senses. And the exquisite sensation of being inside of a woman was worth any amount of aggravation it took to get there.

And here was one waiting for him when he got home, like a birthday present, already half unwrapped. The depression still had him feeling sluggish and angry, but a surprise like this was a reason to live another day, perhaps.

Eric sat down on the leather ottoman near the chair and waited for his eyes to adjust to the dim light. He wanted a closer look at her before she woke up. Who is this gorgeous creature? He studied her long dark hair hanging over her shoulders and curling in tiny ringlets around her face. Her thick eyelashes resting on a lovely oval face. The fine mouth and nose. Her full breasts only minimally covered by the lace on the teddy. The chill in the room making her nipples press out against the silk. Her small hand hanging gracefully over the end of the arm rest.

He turned on the lamp on the side table, removed the headphones from her head and set them aside. She awoke slowly, blinking and moaning softly. It almost sounded like little cat noises.

"When my eyes and brain registered that there was a man sitting in front of me on the ottoman," she told Jack, "I shrieked in terror and jumped standing up on the chair. Eric tried to reassure me that I was safe. He backed away with his palms up in surrender, but I was even more hysterical when he stood up. Eric was six feet six, 265 pounds, broad shouldered and very muscular. He was a scary giant. I was in a complete panic about what this intruder might do to me!"

Stuttering and shaking her hands at him, she jumped off the chair and ran out of the office, her long hair flying, still screaming and looking for any escape.

She ran into the family room before realizing that it was a dead end. She turned around to run again, but Eric ran in after her. He turned on a small goose neck reading lamp, aimed the light at her and closed the door behind him. She was trapped! She reached for the fireplace poker. "Don't you come near me!" she warned, brandishing the poker like a sword. The lamplight was dim and aimed away from the man, so she couldn't get a good look at him, except that he was huge.

"I won't," he chuckled. His voice was deep. He slowly pulled up a chair and sat down in front of the door, blocking her escape. He had snared a wild creature and he was enjoying this little game. Eric had hunted, killed, skinned, cooked and eaten wild creatures, but this was the first one he wanted to take to bed.

He crossed his long legs confidently and smiled at her. "You stay over there on that side of the room. I'll stay over here and we can talk." The half-naked girl was trembling from fear and the chill in the room. "There is a wool lap blanket on the wing-back chair by the fireplace if you would like to sit there and cover up."

"So what am I going to do with this little stray cat?" he thought to himself.

The cat sees a human as a predator and a threat. It will claw and bite if necessary to escape danger. Speak softly to the cat, but do not try to get close or touch the animal while it is frightened. Despite its small size, it can inflict painful injuries.

Eric spoke slowly and in a low voice so that she would calm down. She backed slowly toward the chair, keeping the poker aimed at Eric. Wrapping the lap blanket around herself like a shawl, she stood behind the high back chair for extra cover and protection.

"Who are you?" she demanded sharply. "How did you get into my house? My father is due home about now, so you better get out while you can." She stuck her chin out and spoke with arrogance and authority.

Eric was amused. "My name is Eric and I got in with my front door key. I own the house and I'm sure I'm not your father."

Rosalie drew in a deep breath. "OH!" she cried in dismay. "I, I thought you were a burglar or a killer or something. You scared me to death!"

"I'm not going to hurt you," he said with his hands up. "I just want to talk to you, that's all. You know my name. I'm Eric. What's *your* name?" He tried to sound friendly.

"Rose."

"Why are you sleeping in my house, Rose?"

"Why did you come home *early*, Eric?" she demanded angrily.

Eric laughed out loud at this surprising show of bravado. *"Fearless, defiant, cocky,"* he thought with a smile. *"Interesting woman."*

"I came home early because I wasn't having any fun. Why are *you* here?"

"I wasn't having fun out there either," she said, trying not to cry.

"Out where?"

"On the streets, where I live."

"Umm. Homeless." Eric bought a lot of expensive lingerie for ladies over the years, and the silk teddy Rose was wearing was nothing a homeless woman could afford. A boyfriend bought it or she stole it. "Were you planning to rob the place?"

"No," she lied. "I go into empty houses where I can eat and sleep for a night when it's cold out. I thought I really lucked out when I saw on your calendar you'd be gone for a week. I did eat your food while you were gone."

"There are homeless shelters," he said. "Breaking into houses and stealing food could land you in jail."

"Are you going to call the cops?"

"I haven't decided yet." He had no intention of calling the cops, but he was intrigued and wanted to drag this out for a while longer. This babe was smokin' hot and he planned to coax her out of that teddy before the night was over. "Have you done this sort of thing before? Breaking into houses for food and a place to sleep?"

Rosalie nodded.

"And you've never been caught?"

"No. I clean up and don't leave any signs of a break-in, except for a little food that people don't usually miss. I don't damage anything."

She was babbling fast to buy time and think of a way out of this predicament.

CAMPING SAFETY

The best way to avoid being mauled by a bear is to stay out of the bear's habitat. If you encounter a bear, don't do anything threatening. Back away slowly. Give the bear room to walk away.

"Talk nice to the big bear. Smile. Don't piss him off. Put away the weapon." She put the poker back by the fireplace and kept talking. She had left her paring knife in her jeans in the housekeeper's room, but it probably wouldn't have been much help against this big bear anyway. She couldn't do much to stop him, no matter what he decided to do tonight.

"The people don't call the cops because they don't know that I was ever there. I would have left everything neat and clean here, too, before I left. If you let me dress and get my stuff, I'll clear out. I haven't damaged anything here, you can check. I would be very grateful if you just let me go and not call the cops. I'll clean up the mess in the kitchen before I go."

He folded his arms and looked at her thoughtfully, deciding that she was a career burglar with a very good angle that had worked for her in the past. If she ever got caught, she posed as a pitiful homeless woman who could talk the homeowners into giving her a few dollars and sandwiches for the road. "I can't imagine how a woman as beautiful as you could be homeless. Not even a boyfriend to take care of you?"

"It's not safe to depend on a man. It's better to be homeless."

That comment had the ring of truth. "Safe? Men have mistreated her in the past, but she won't take it anymore. Or is she lying again? Maybe the boyfriend is in this with her."

"You seem to be intelligent enough to get a job and a place to stay. Why haven't you?"

"You can't get a job anywhere without a Social Security card and you can't get that without a birth certificate and you can't get that without fifteen dollars. Which I don't have. And I don't have a high school education either. So my job prospects are pretty slim."

"You sound well-educated for a high school dropout," he said, doubting her every word.

"I never made it to high school. My grand-mother paid for me to go to a good Catholic school from first grade on. I got a good education while it lasted."

"Why did you quit?"

"My grandmother died. I live on my own now."

"I'm sorry to hear that. You have no other relatives?"

"None that are … safe," she said softly.

Eric nodded, understanding the meaning of that completely. "You are the bravest, smartest and most beautiful stray cat I have ever met," he said with genuine appreciation. "I would like to help you get on your feet, if you like. You're welcome to stay here. I won't have you arrested. Think of it as an upscale homeless shelter for one. This is a big house and I would welcome the company of a lovely young woman for the holidays. Besides, I can't put you out on the street at Thanksgiving. That would be uncivilized."

HOW TO TAME A FERAL CAT
(Continued)

Do not try to approach the cat. Allow the animal to come close to you on its own. Offer the cat some food, a toy or other treat.

"Here kitty, kitty, kitty. Kitty want a treat? I have something nice for you."

"After the holidays, if you choose to stay, I can help you get the birth certificate and Social Security card you need and help you find a job. Or, you can stay longer while you get your GED, then find a job and an apartment you can afford. You won't have to break into houses after that. You won't be homeless. That is, if it sounds like something you'd like." He stood up, returned the chair to its original spot and opened the door. "But you're free to leave tonight if you want to."

He thought the offer would be too good to pass up, if her story was true. Portraying himself as a nice, generous benefactor, he was confident that he could woo her to his bed in time. Eric didn't have any qualms about taking advantage of a woman in distress. He never pretended to be a white knight.

On the other hand, he thought, she might be a common street criminal who would steal whatever she can and sneak out during the night. But what the hell? Life is short and this could be fun.

She was offended when he called her a stray cat. But he could insult her freely because he could have her arrested, if he wanted to. "Why would you do this for a perfect stranger?"

"Why not? I'd hate to think of you ending up in jail or being shot by an angry homeowner."

And as for the pretense of his "generous offer," Rose understood how guys are. *Nothing's free. You gotta give it up, girl, if you want to stay here. Might as well cut the crap and get on with it.*

"You'd expect me to sleep with you?"

"Of course," he said very softly, trying not to sound surprised at how easy his plan was working out. "But this is a really nice place, my housekeeper Evelyn is a great cook and you can have a lovely bedroom and bath of your own. I won't be unkind to you. If we get along well and you like staying here, you can stay a while and leave whenever you want. We part as friends, owing each other nothing. I wouldn't expect anything perverted, just normal missionary sex. Do you like sex, Rose?"

"Not really. It's never been much fun."

"I'm sorry to hear that," he said sincerely.

She considered her options. "Have sex with this rich guy, who might be a hateful, selfish bastard like all the others. Or, take a chance that he'll be a nice guy after all and you get to live in a mansion and eat well. Or, leave now, become homeless again and have sex occasionally with guys you pick up who have crummy little apartments and order take-out pizza. He wants me to live here, so the old guy probably has trouble getting girls. Maybe that gives me some bargaining power.”

“Well,” she hesitated, “I’ll stay for a while, I guess. I appreciate the offer. You seem like a nice guy. But we should treat this as a business arrangement,” she said in a business-like manner, hoping to tip the power imbalance in her favor. Show no fear. Get the upper hand. Don’t act like a victim. “We already agree on the basics. You provide a place to stay and I provide sex. There are other issues, of course, to be negotiated.”

“Issues? Negotiated? Like hell,” he thought, feeling pissed off. He narrowed his eyes at her.

“I’m sure you’re tired after your long trip, so let’s both get a good night’s sleep and work out the details tomorrow,” she said cheerily. “Goodnight, Mr. Weber. I’ve been sleeping in the housekeeper’s room, but I’ll move into one of the guest rooms tomorrow.” She tossed the wool shawl on the chair and breezed past him with all the confidence of a corporate CEO leaving a board meeting, all the while trembling inside and hoping her bluff paid off.

“Hmpf. That smartass little twit breaks into my house, threatens me with a poker and then brazenly expects me to negotiate terms for my own surrender! Well, that ain’t gonna happen, Sweet Cheeks.”

“Hold on there, Rose,” he called to her gently. He came up behind her and caught her by the shoulders. He slid the straps of the teddy off her tiny shoulders and it slipped to her feet.

“OH!” she cried out in surprise, instinctively clutching her arms to her naked breasts.

If the cat comes near you for a treat or toy, do not try to touch the head or front of the animal at first. That would frighten the cat, who would take it as a sign of aggression. Pet only the tail end until the cat is comfortable with you.

Eric hadn't noticed it before, but Rose had the finest little butt he had ever seen on a white girl. It was high and round like ripe fruit. He turned her around to face him, picked her up over his shoulder fireman style and carried her wide-eyed and naked up the stairs. "You already owe me for three days room and board. We'll settle that account tonight and discuss the other details tomorrow."

Eric squinted his eyes and smirked to himself as he climbed the long wide stairs to his bedroom. "Who's got the upper hand, now, you arrogant little alley cat? I'm going to bang you until you can't see straight."

As she hung naked, upside down, six feet in the air and terrified about what this giant psycho might do to her, she reconsidered her decision to stay.

"If I survive the night, I'll collect my stuff and sneak out of the house as soon as the old dude falls asleep. Oh, sweet Jesus! What is he going to do to me?"

CHAPTER 18

Eric pulled back the covers and put Rose in his bed. She turned her head away and wouldn't look at him. He was a scary guy. Cold as ice, arrogant and *strong*.

CAMPING SAFETY
(Continued)

If you are unable to escape from the bear and it approaches you, play dead. Don't make eye contact.

He lit the gas fireplace to warm the room. He didn't turn on the bedroom lights, got undressed in the dark and slipped into bed next to her. He didn't have to touch her to sense how tiny she was, compared to the women he usually had.

Eric dated tall thin women exclusively. Preferably supermodels. He liked to hold a woman in his arms he could easily talk to or kiss without bending over to reach her.

He had a certain reputation as an amazing lover and women were always eager to join him in bed. Rose wasn't. She was stiff and frightened, but tried not to show it. She looked stoic, resigned to her fate. But she held on to the hope that he wouldn't be violent, because this house would be a great place to stay, like a big luxury hotel.

"If he doesn't try to pull any 'Fifty Shades of Eric' on me, I might stay here. It would be nice to stay in one place for a while."

****

Rose chose to keep secret the details of that first night with Eric. Jack wouldn't understand how she could actually enjoy having sex with a stranger who took advantage of her situation so coldly. All she said about it was that she and Eric slept together and he was kind to her.

As she sipped more of her coffee and gathered her thoughts, she remembered what a spectacular lover he was …

****

A voice spoke to Eric that only he could hear. "You can save her and she can save you," the voice whispered gently. Eric shook his head to dispel the message. It shocked him. *"Hearing voices now? Is that part of it? Will the tumor make me psychotic, too?"*

Eric tried to forget about the voice, but it changed his thinking about Rose. He did himself no favors by scaring her the way he did. He would rather have her participate with enthusiasm and not lie there like a rock. He pulled the covers over her, stroked her hair gently away from her face and spoke very softly and seductively to her while waiting for the room to warm up.

"I apologize for treating you so roughly. That was rude of me. I'm sorry, honestly. I would like for you to feel safe and enjoy staying here. I said that I wouldn't hurt you and I meant it. We'll take our time. Rose, you said that you didn't particularly like sex?"

She still didn't look at him, just shrugged with feigned indifference.

"I'd like to change that for you, if I can. Show you that it can be wonderful with someone who wants to give you pleasure."

She turned and looked at him, confused. "What's he up to? He doesn't have to seduce me. I'm already here in his bed. Maybe he just wants me to let my guard down."

"Have you ever had an orgasm during sex?" She shook her head. "If you will relax and trust me not to hurt you in any way, I would like to go slowly and pleasure every part of your body, from top to bottom, giving careful attention to every important stop along the way. May I start with a good back rub to help you relax?"

This was definitely not what she expected. She didn't respond or resist when he rolled her over gently, leaving just the sheet around her. Nobody had ever given her a back massage before. No man had ever been concerned with her pleasure, except for the ones who occasionally asked afterwards if she enjoyed it. She always lied and said yes.

Eric started at her neck and shoulders, and as he skillfully and patiently worked his way down her back, kissing and nibbling and massaging away her muscle tension with his strong hands, he pushed the sheet down, uncovering her back, buttocks and thighs slowly an inch at a time. She couldn't help but moan and sink into the mattress, too relaxed to be afraid.

When he was done with the back of her body and the sheet was gone, he rolled her over gently and began to work his way down her front, starting with kissing her face and mouth. She didn't want to respond, but *damn* he was a great kisser! His kiss was deep and thorough. Passionate, but not rough like some guys. He nibbled tenderly on her lips, ears and throat. It was so good, her body felt like it was buzzing all over. Eric didn't go any further down until she wrapped her arms around his neck and moaned for more. As he had with the back of her body, he slowly worked his way down the front, kissing and nibbling and massaging all of her tender parts until she was moaning and writhing under him.

Eric was a superior lover with an unrelenting appetite for sex. He took pride in being skilled at thawing out the frigid, seducing the unwary, surprising even the jaded and initiating virgins. In some ways, he was like a great musician. He had a *very* fine instrument for making music between a man and a woman. He also used his lips and tongue, hands and fingers to bring out the sweetest sounds from his partner. Deep low moans early on. Then mid-range oh-oh-oh's as the intensity builds. And finally, the long, loud, high-pitched cries of ecstasy when his mouth and fingers reach the tiny pearl of paradise, concealed inside her like a precious treasure. He took Rose there twice and made her wet and ready for him before he slipped inside.

Both of them cried out in surprise when he did. Rose, because he was so big. Eric, because she was so tight. He took it slow and easy until she was comfortable with him and matched his hip thrusts with her own.

After they both came, Eric asked her if she liked sex. He could feel the muscles inside her tremble and spasm with pleasure when she came, so he knew she wasn't faking it. But he wanted her to say it.

"That *was* good. Really good." This time, she meant it. When the bear wrapped his arms under her and pulled her tight against his body, she felt like she had no will of her own and didn't care. It was amazing to just lose herself completely in the experience.

"Rest a while, and we'll try to make it even better next time," he said, wrapping his long muscular arms around her and pulling her back to his chest, so they were nestled together like spoons.

"Better?" she murmured as she wondered if her heart would ever stop pounding. "What could be better than that?"

Eric smiled. "Wait and see." As soon as he recovered, he woke her, kissing and fondling her breasts. She responded by giving herself to him freely and fully, running her hands through his hair and moaning with pleasure. She knew what to expect this time and was eager for him to do whatever he wanted.

When they were done the second time, they couldn't let go of each other. "You were right," she moaned, struggling to breathe. "It *was* better!" Eric did not withdraw from her body, wanting more of her as quickly as possible. She did, too. She wrapped her legs around his hips and arched her back to hold him there. They continued to kiss and press against each other with so much hunger that both were ready for more in minutes. They were insatiable.

The third time was explosive. She gave herself to the pleasure completely, holding nothing back, while Eric dove into her like a mad man. He could hardly believe how different she was. How she responded immediately with so much hunger, passion and energy. How she drove him crazy like no woman ever had before. They reached fulfillment together, and still wrapped in each other's arms, fell into exhausted sleep immediately.

Rose woke up around nine o'clock in the morning when Eric got out of bed. In the daylight, she got her first good look at Eric's magnificent face and body. Every inch of him was toned and muscular, not like a body builder, but like an athlete. Not an ounce of fat anywhere, just hard round muscles. He walked around the room gathering up his dirty clothes and putting them in his laundry basket, completely comfortable being naked. His back and shoulders were about a mile wide and he filled up the doorway when he went to his walk-in closet. He was nicely tanned and his thick, sandy blond hair was streaked by the sun. There wasn't much body hair, just a bit of pale blond fuzz at the center of his chest.

Rose didn't speak, but continued watching him as he gathered his workout clothes for the day. Tossing his clean clothes on a chair, he walked slowly over to the bed, giving Rose an unobstructed view of his impressive manhood. Even in a relaxed state, it made Rose catch her breath. The big guy was big all over.

"Whoa!" she thought. "No wonder I'm hurting! He's a horse!"

"Are you going to get up today?" he asked casually, his voice deep and intimate. He sat down on the bed next to her.

"I can't move," she moaned. She rubbed her face into the puffy feather pillow, enjoying the feel of the soft expensive sheets.

"Did I hurt you, Rose? You did a lot of yelling, but I thought it was from pleasure, not pain," he teased.

Eric was as handsome as any movie star. He had a killer smile, green eyes and a strong jaw line. When he lowered his head and glanced at her sideways, her heart flipped and her body began to buzz all over again. As much as her body ached, she was hoping he would come back to bed.

"It was pleasure. It was *definitely* pleasure," she said with a dreamy smile. "I don't think I'll be able to walk for days."

"If you can't walk, then I'll carry you." Both of them still naked, he picked her up and carried her to the last guest room at the end of the hall. "This will be your private room while you're here. When you wake up later, soak in a tub of hot water for a while and the muscle soreness will go away. Your private bathroom is through that door." Without another word or smile, he put her in the bed, covered her up and closed her door when he left. He went back to his room to dress.

She felt offended. "He's done with me for now, so he disposed of me like I was a used condom. He's gorgeous and incredible in bed, but it'll still be hard to tolerate the arrogant prick." Before she fell asleep, a scary thought came to her and she opened her eyes wide in shock. Eric didn't use a condom. "Oh, shit!"

Eric didn't feel happy about leaving her alone either. What he really wanted was to crawl back in bed and spend all day there with her. To taste her mouth and breasts and thighs again and feel how tight she was when he thrust deep inside of her. To feel her respond. To run his hands through her long hair or feel it tickle his face and chest.

But he couldn't let himself be that vulnerable with her. He was the "love 'em and leave 'em" kind of man. Instead, he got dressed, worked out in his equipment room for an hour, then made himself a pot of coffee and some toast.

Rose slept in her room until mid-afternoon. Her clean clothes were still in the housekeeper's room where she left them the night before, so she borrowed another large tee shirt from Eric's closet to wear downstairs. She found Eric at the dining table drinking coffee and reading the newspaper.

CHAPTER 19

He waited impatiently for her to come downstairs. Her hair was a wild tangle and she was barefooted. She looked so sexy that it took his breath away.

"My cook and housekeeper won't be back from vacation until Monday. Since I wasn't planning to be here, she went to spend Thanksgiving and the weekend with her married daughter in Baton Rouge. We'll go out for Thanksgiving dinner later this evening," he said. It sounded more like an order than an invitation. "Help yourself to some breakfast, if you like."

Rose brought both orange juice and coffee to the dining room, and went back to the kitchen for a sliced apple, buttered toast and a bowl of cornflakes. "When your housekeeper gets back, would she make us some French toast and pancakes and stuff like that for breakfast?"

"I'm sure she would. You'll just need to tell her what you want," he said without looking up from his newspaper.

"Good. Because I can build up a big appetite after a workout in bed with *you*!"

Eric hid his face behind the newspaper and struggled not to laugh out loud at her honesty.

He hardly spoke to her for the rest of the day, busying himself with phone calls and work at his desk and trying not to think about last night. The girl got under his skin and he didn't like it. He couldn't look at her or think about her without being aroused again. No woman was going to drive him crazy like that, or have that power over him. He had to keep his distance and be cool. As she said, this was a business arrangement.

While Eric worked in his office, Rose explored every room in the house with lights on for the first time. The great room was as beautiful all lit up as she imagined it would be. She stood out on the front porch in the daylight and admired the gardens in the back yard. Someone had raked and bagged leaves recently, leaving the bags lined up against the garage. All of the flower beds and lawn were perfectly groomed and decorated with fall blooming perennials of gold, orange, red and purple. As the sun was going down, the air was too chilly to linger outside. She went inside to dress for her Thanks-giving dinner out with Eric.

Rose wore a white cashmere sweater and a soft leather mini skirt to dinner. They were both taken from previous house sittings. She thought she looked very respectable, not like she had ever been hungry or homeless. She wanted Eric to be pleased, but he had nothing to say and barely glanced at her.

Eric tried to avoid looking at her luscious body. Those thighs barely covered by the mini skirt had been wrapped around his hips last night. And the way that sweater showed off her generous breasts! He didn't want to walk into a crowded restaurant with a huge erection and lust in his eyes.

Rose had learned to recognize high quality clothes from her friend Steven and appreciated the way Eric looked in them. He wore an impeccably tailored dark blue wool suit, an expensive tie and a white silk shirt that clung to his pectoral muscles. The French cuffs were adorned with his initials and gold cufflinks. He normally didn't make any special effort to dress up just to go out to dinner in town, not for any woman, but for some reason he couldn't explain, he wanted to impress Rose. *"I can't believe I'm being such an idiot over a common thief!"*

Rose was impressed indeed at the figure waiting downstairs for her. He looked even bigger in a suit. He had a casual way of standing that made him look so tempting she wanted to jump into his arms. He was freshly shaved and smelling like paradise.

"He's as beautiful and perfect as a golden god," she thought. "He never had trouble getting women, that's for sure. So why ask me to stay here?"

Arnaud's was the nicest restaurant Rose had ever been in. Chandeliers, white tablecloths, the wall of mirrors and everything. Everyone was dressed up, even the waiters. The restaurant maître d' greeted his frequent dinner guest warmly. "Mr. Weber! So glad you're back in town."

"Thank you, André. It's good to see you again. Can you get us a table without a reservation? We didn't expect to be in town."

"No problem at all. It's not very crowded tonight," André said with a big smile.

Drayton, the waiter, also greeted Eric like an old friend. "Do you recommend the Thanksgiving turkey tonight, Dray?"

"Confidentially," the waiter said in a low voice, leaning close, "the roast duck is much better. It's *very* special today. Leave the turkey to the tourists." Eric chuckled and ordered the duck and all the trimmings for both of them, plus a good wine. Eric didn't ask Rose what she wanted. She thought it was rude of him, but it was his ticket, after all.

Surprised, she was amazed with the duck! She had never eaten food like this before, and she savored every bite from turtle soup and shrimp salad to the crème brûleé. Even the warm, crusty French bread with real butter was special. She told Eric the dinner was really good, except for the wine. She would have preferred a Pepsi. Eric choked back a laugh under his napkin and told the waiter to bring her a Pepsi.

"Interesting woman," he thought. "She's as wanton as a mistress one minute and as honest as a child the next."

They didn't talk much over dinner, because a steady stream of fans and friends kept coming over to their table to say hello and to meet Eric's dinner companion.

"You're pretty famous, huh?" she asked over dessert, trying not to sound impressed. Eric shrugged as though it were no big deal.

"Why did you become a writer?"

"My parents both passed away when I was in college. My father and grandfather both left me a generous inheritance, so I didn't plan to look for a job after school. I wanted to travel around the world. I was talking to a college friend about some of my travel adventures and he said I should write a book about it. I created a fictional hero named Cade Monroe and some nasty villains to go with him, and it became a best seller. Now, when I go someplace interesting, I try to decide what kind of adventure or danger the brave hero might have there."

When they returned home from Thanksgiving dinner, Eric took off his coat and tie, let his shirt hang out and relaxed in the family room to catch the news and football games on television. She didn't like Eric's company all that much, except in bed, so she kept her distance. Rose went to the little sitting room, lit the fireplace and turned on some soft music.

She liked the XM channel that played old love songs she had never heard before. They were kind of sweet and innocent, different from the music she heard in clubs and bars. Eric came in later to see if she was okay, and heard the slow guitar instrumental *Maria Elena* playing. "I really love that old song. Would you dance with me?"

Rose took his hand and let him hold her close as they danced. Her right hand disappeared in his big paw, with the left resting on his hard biceps. He smelled wonderful, not with cologne, but the actual smell of his clean, warm, masculine body. He felt so strong and protective, she had to resist the urge to rest her head on his chest. She longed to feel that safe, for once in her life, but in spite of their intimacy in bed, she hardly knew him.

Eric could feel the muscle tension in her body. "Alvarez is Spanish," he said softly as they danced. "Where's your family from originally?" He thought casual conversation would help both of them to relax.

"I'm not Mexican," she said defensively. "My grandmother told me that our family came here from Spain a long time ago. My mother was Cajun French, so I guess I'm a mixture."

"A very lovely mixture." Dancing with her in his arms, he realized, had not been a good idea. His shirt hanging out hid his growing arousal, but he had to hold her a safe distance from his hips to keep her from brushing against him. He wanted her to think he was cool and calm.

"Where are *your* people from?" she asked.

"My dad was a tall German from old Viking stock. That's where I get my blond hair and love of adventure. Blame everything on our genes," he added in a mumble. "The good and the bad."

"The fault, dear Brutus, lies not in our stars *or* ourselves, but in our genes. That's a popular post-Christian philosophy," she said very seriously, looking up to his face.

Shakespeare and philosophy? Rose never ceased to surprise him. "I suppose that's what I am. A post-Christian," he said wearily.

When the song ended, he leaned down and kissed the top of her head. "Thank you for the dance," he said as he walked away.

"It's getting late. Shouldn't we sit down and discuss our business agreement tonight?" she asked.

"It's a holiday, and I've had too much food and wine. We'll negotiate tomorrow," he said, and went back to the family room and television to let the swelling in his pants settle down.

"Poor old dude. Last night wore him out. I wonder how old he is?" she thought.

To her surprise, when he was ready for bed, he came and took her by the hand to his bedroom. "Um … how often do you want me to have sex with you?" she asked as he slowly and gently undressed her at his bedside.

"Whenever I want it," he said in an off-hand way, as he slid her skirt and panties off. No emotion, no seductive words, like he was unwrapping a brown paper package. But he was hurting for her in the worst way.

"It's okay with me if he wants it every night. He is so damned good! I just hope the old guy doesn't have a stroke," she thought.

Eric was thinking the same thing. "This girl is going to give me a heart attack. But it's a great way to go!"

With only brief foreplay, Rose was wet and ready for him. He was surprised when she pulled him to her and guided him inside. It took all of his strength to hold off for her to come first. "I'm sorry I came so fast," he said panting.

"Are you too tired to do it again?" she asked sweetly.

"Oh, hell no," he laughed. "I won't quit until you're satisfied or I keel over and die in your arms." Their second night together was better than the first.

On Friday, Eric went to the post office, collected his mail and went right to his office to pay the bills. Rose was in the room ahead of him, listening to his music, singing and dancing around with abandon. She didn't notice him come in. Eric leaned his shoulder on the door frame, crossed his arms and silently watched her entertain herself. She was mesmerizing. He couldn't help but smile. She stopped when she turned and saw him.

"If you have work to do, I'll turn it off and leave you alone," she offered.

"No, stay. And leave the music on. It's nice. I'm just going to check my e-mail, read the snail mail and pay some bills."

She sat and watched him at his desk. He looked so serious opening the stack of mail, writing checks and stamping envelopes. He paid most of his bills on line. "Do you have enough money to pay all your bills at one time?"

"Yes, I do," he laughed.

"I never knew anybody who could do that. It must be nice to be rich."

He quit working and smiled at her. "What would you do if you were rich?"

"Oh, man! I would have a closet full of clothes. Designer labels only, not the cheap stuff. And silky lingerie in every color. I would fly off to exciting places and do all kinds of fun things. I would eat anything I wanted. I would have a home of my own and live like normal people. I would be respectable enough to marry a nice guy and have a few kids. I would help my friends, too. But … I don't need to be rich to be happy," she said, dismissing the impossible fantasy with a wave of her hand. "I would be happy if I could get my GED, a decent job and an apartment."

"You're a smart girl, Rose. After you get your GED, you should consider college. With a degree, you could make even bigger dreams come true. A good-paying job, a home of your own, nice clothes." She continued to think about college as an actual goal for the first time. *"'Dream big' he said."*

She slapped her own knee when the bright idea came to her. "I would like to go to college," she said, "but that takes money. That's why you'll need to pay me a salary for my services as your Research Assistant!"

CHAPTER 20

Rose didn't tell Jack the details of the bargaining session she had with Eric. All she said was that she would be travelling with Eric and might as well be useful to him in his work. He could pay her a small salary which she would save until she started college. And Eric generously agreed. Yeah, well, that wasn't exactly the way it happened …

****

"My Research Assistant? When did you become my Research Assistant?" Eric exclaimed.

"Well, think about it Eric," she said. "I'm not your mistress or your girlfriend, because both of those imply some kind of affectionate relationship. I'm your employee. I provide a specific service. Meals and housing are not payment for my services. I'm on call 24/7 and I'm required to be close at hand if my services are needed. Living and eating here are a requirement of the job. It's like being a fireman, ya' know? They sleep and eat at the firehouse because they have to. I deserve a salary for my services and some kind of respectable job title in case people ask who I am and why I'm living here."

Eric stared at her seriously and shook his head in amazement at how she turned a simple living arrangement into a career plan. "Have you ever had your IQ tested?"

"Yes."

"What was it?"

"None of your business."

He nodded, still eyeing her seriously. An eighth grade education and the mind of a lawyer. Superior range or higher, probably?

"Alright, let's negotiate our employment agreement today," he said, sounding all business-like. Matching wits with her was entertaining, like playing chess. He handed her a sheet of paper and a pen. "Write down your terms and I'll write down mine. We'll see where we agree and where we need further discussion."

"Excellent," Rose said with a nod and began to write.

When they both put their pens down, Eric asked, "Shall we begin with your expected salary?"

"Seven hundred a week," she said without batting an eyelash.

"WHAT?" he shouted, almost choking. "Not a chance! That's a completely unreasonable demand. We have to negotiate in good faith, Rose."

"I'll explain why it's more than reasonable. In fact, it's a bargain. A guy wants sex seven days a week, if he can get it. Right?"

"Naturally," he agreed.

"An important guy like you, if you want sex with a woman, you don't just make a booty call. You take her out to dinner. If you don't take her someplace nice, she might be disappointed and refuse to have sex with a cheapskate. Dinner would cost you at least a hundred bucks, with wine. Daily sex would cost you about seven hundred bucks a week.”

“Why go out to someplace expensive when I could invite a lady here for dinner? Evelyn is a great cook.”

“Bringing a lady here for an overnight could get complicated. You have to get her out of your house in the morning or she might start to feel possessive. She’ll expect you to call her and send flowers and stuff like that. Why put up with that just to get laid?”

“I’m willing to put up with some inconvenience,” he said. “The thrill of the chase can be fun, too.”

“For zero inconvenience, you could hire a prostitute to come here. A good one would cost you at least a hundred. Blow job might be extra. If she spends the whole night you’d have to pay at least three hundred. With me, you get guaranteed sex, when you want it, as often as you want it, for a flat rate of seven hundred a week. There are other benefits as well. You don’t need to buy me flowers or presents. I won’t nag you for a commitment like a girlfriend would. You can tell me to leave at any time. You don’t have to dress up or go out in all kinds of weather to meet a lady. But if you need variety, you still keep the option of sleeping with ladies away from home without any drama from me. Monogamy is not expected. Of course, sex with them probably wouldn’t be as good as it is with me.” She smiled and coyly batted her lashes at him.

Eric glared at her in silence. “You should be a labor union negotiator.”

Rose smiled and waited. “Well?”

"She's flirting. I'll try intimidation. This makes even tough guys back down in a barroom brawl. I could make football players wet their pants when they saw me coming at them on the field." He crossed his arms, set his jaw, tilted his head slightly to one side and glared a hole straight through her.

"Four hundred a week," he said. It was pocket change to him. The sex was worth a lot more, but he wanted to win.

She rolled her eyes at him. "Get serious. You know the value of my services, Eric." She stared at him for a while, but he didn't blink.

"Okay, here's a counter offer. I used to get the clothes I needed by taking them from houses where I was staying for a night. If I stay here, I can't do that anymore. Provide me with a decent wardrobe so I can attend GED classes and I'll take five hundred a week."

"Three hundred. Spend your own money to buy clothes." His voice was so deep it was almost a growl.

"Goodbye, Mr. Weber," Rose said cheerfully with a smile as she stood up. "It was a sincere pleasure meeting you, but I'll go upstairs and pack my things and go now." She went upstairs to her room, scooped her few belongings into the large tote that served as her purse and luggage, and headed downstairs.

Eric met her halfway on the stairs, tossed her over his shoulder again and carried her up to his bedroom. "We are done negotiating, Eric!" she yelled at him upside down. "We are not going to have sex. I'm LEAVING!"

He slapped her hard on the butt and she cursed at him. "ALRIGHT!" he yelled back at her. "You'll get your damned five hundred and a wardrobe," he said sullenly. He had been out-talked by an alley cat and it hurt his ego. He kicked his bedroom door closed hard with a slam and tossed Rose onto the bed like a sack of potatoes. She held out her arms to him with a satisfied *cat-that-ate-the-canary* smile.

He crawled into bed without bothering to undress either one of them, just removing the obstructions enough to satisfy his need as quickly as possible. Rose undressed herself and Eric when he was done. "Now it's *my* turn," she said, rolling him into her arms.

Rose took a big gamble. The labor walkout could have become a management lockout. But for the time being, Eric was controlled by lust and intrigued by this little spitfire.

Rose woke up and looked at the clock on the bedside table. Eric was wrapped around her back. She rolled away from him and shook him awake. "Hey. We skipped lunch and it's five o'clock. I'm starved! Let's get some food." She got up and dressed.

"Go down to the kitchen and fix us something," he mumbled.

"My duties end at the bedroom, Mr. Weber. I don't cook or clean or do windows."

He reached for her from the bed, but she dodged him with a giggle and went downstairs. They went out for cheeseburgers and fries, then resumed negotiations in his office.

"What other terms do you want to discuss? You expect a company car, a 401(k) and a dental plan?"

"No, and you don't have to be so snarky," she said with a smile. "I want to be excused from work to attend my GED classes. I'll find out where, when, how long the classes are and all that. Plus time on public transit both ways. If homework or study are required, I'll need time for that, too."

"Agreed. That's a reasonable request. I'm sure it won't require a dissertation. Anything else?"

"After I get the GED, I want to apply for college as a part-time student instead of looking for a job. I'll have savings from my salary here to cover some of the costs and I can apply for financial aid. But I'll need half days off to go to classes. Getting my degree will take some time, but you said I could stay here indefinitely. I know you can change your mind and not want me to stay that long. So that's okay, too. It's not personal, it's just business."

"Hmm. Keeping up with college classes might be a problem, Rose. One of my terms for your employment is that you will travel with me when I leave home overnight. Phone sex ain't gonna cut it for me."

"Okay, well, I can do makeup classes for the GED. For college classes, I can get a student to tell me what I missed. I can work around your travel schedule. Where do you go?"

"All over the country for publicity tours and all over the world for story ideas."

Her eyes were wide and she was stunned. "You want to take me with you ... all over the *world*?"

"And since you will be my Research Assistant, I will require you to be my photographer when I'm working on a new book. In whatever country we go to, you will photograph the native culture, flora and fauna, landmarks, buildings and scenery that might be useful in the story line."

"Yeah, you bet," she said, still amazed at the prospect of being a world traveler. "I, I guess I should practice with a camera before we go anywhere.”

He opened a desk drawer and pulled out his Nikon camera. It was big, old and heavy. “I’m not looking for art, just good documentation. The camera focuses itself. All you have to do is hold it steady and push the button.”

“This camera takes better pictures than you need, and it isn’t very convenient for travelling,” she said, handing it back to him. “Get me a smart phone instead. I can do photography, research and communications all in one device that’ll fit in my pocket. Do you have any other items on your list for us to discuss?” she asked.

“Yes. You will not bring friends here. Even though this will be your home, I don’t want strangers in the house.”

“Agreed,” she said. “Anything else?”

“When other people are present, here or out in public, you will refer to me respectfully as Mr. Weber, your employer, and you will act profession- ally like a Research Assistant should. I will refer to you as Ms. Alvarez.”

“Agreed,” she said. “I have two more things. First, if you bring a woman here, call ahead and let me know and I’ll stay out of sight. Second, don’t ever hit me again. That hurt. You are too big to be hitting on someone my size.”

“I agree, of course,” he said contritely. He was embarrassed that he needed to be reminded of that. “Anything else?”

“Yes. I’m not on the pill and you didn’t use a condom. Aren’t you concerned about protection?”

“I had a vasectomy twenty years ago. No wife, no kids, not ever. You didn’t worry about protection either.”

"Yeah, well, you swept me off my feet," she said.

CHAPTER 21

Eric's housekeeper was in the kitchen Monday morning when Eric and Rose got up, lured from bed early by the smell of fresh coffee and breakfast cooking.

"May I present Mrs. Evelyn Dunn and Ms. Rose Alvarez," he said with a nod to each. "Mrs. Dunn has been my housekeeper since I was in college and I can't get along without her," he said. "Rose will be living here," he said to Evelyn.

As they ate breakfast at the big table in the dining room, Rose asked Eric, "What would you like to do today? Got any plans?"

"Yes, we need to go downtown and apply for a certified copy of your birth certificate. You'd need that to get a passport and a Social Security card. While you're looking into the GED classes, I'll be making arrangements for us to go to New York in a couple of days. I need to meet with my publisher and we'll be attending an award banquet honoring a friend of mine."

"I don't have any clothes to wear on a trip."

"Wear what you have on the plane and we'll get your school and travel wardrobe in New

York," he said casually as he read the morning paper.

"Clothes from New York City! Hot damn!" she thought with her eyes wide. "I would have been happy with jeans and tee shirts from the mall! But I guess I do need to dress up when I go to fancy places with an important guy like Eric. He wouldn't want me to be an embarrassment."

Eric and Rose went to Vital Records downtown in the Benson Tower for their birth certificates, filled out their forms and waited on uncomfortable molded chairs for the State's computerized system to search for the data. The waiting room was filled with women and their young children, and one young man in a suit. Despite the polite and efficient clerks serving them, some customers were complaining and impatient, because only people in a hurry came in person to get their documents. Everyone else sent for them by mail.

Eric paid the fees and they left with their certified copies. As they were walking back to the car in the Superdome parking garage next door, Rose asked Eric if she could see his birth certificate. "I want to see how old you are," she explained.

"I'll show you mine, if you'll show me yours," he teased suggestively. "I'm forty," he said.

Rose stopped walking and frowned at Eric. "Good grief! I had no idea you were *that* old!" she said seriously.

Eric was offended. "Well, you didn't think I was old in bed," he said with his hands on his hips. "You came three times last night," he bragged, holding up three fingers. "And you quit before I did."

"Yeah, you did good for an old man," she smirked. She gave Eric her birth certificate to look at.

"SEVENTEEN!" Eric shouted when he read it. "Is that right? You're a *child*? Ohhh nooo!" he agonized, holding his head and groaning in misery.

"What's wrong with that?"

Eric leaned against a parked car to steady himself and clutched his heart. "I just missed committing a felony! You look so much more mature, I thought you were at least twenty-one." When he stopped hyperventilating, he said, "Rose, you have to get parental consent to apply for a passport."

"My parents are both dead."

"Then we have to go back to Vital Records and get the death certificates. And when we travel, you can't be just an employee. You're a minor and it would look ... *scandalous*! You'll need to be a relative of some kind."

"Your niece?'

"No. Everybody knows I have no family. No children, brothers or sisters," he said. "You can't be my niece. What's our relationship? Distant cousins?"

"We should stay as close to the truth as possible," Rose said. "Less chance of being tripped up by somebody. How about this. Before you became a post-Christian, you were an actual Christian (true?) and in your younger days you stood as my godfather when I was baptized (possible). After my parents died (true), none of my relatives wanted me (true). You made a solemn vow to your deceased friend that you would take care of his little girl (not likely, but possible), so you did the right thing and took her into your home. As a caring godfather, you never leave the grieving child alone and take her with you in all your travels.”

“And always a two bedroom suite for appearances,” Eric reasoned. “Female friends would understand that I can’t invite them to my bedroom anymore because my godchild is always with me. If at some point we decide not to stay together, I could say that I had to put you in a boarding school because I travel a lot.”

“And a man of your wealth would naturally provide your godchild with an allowance and see to her education,” Rose added, seeing a chance to improve the terms of her employment agreement. “You would be indulgent and generous with her.”

“But, great kid that she is, she insists on ‘earning her keep’ by working as my Research Assistant. This is a very good cover story. I like it. We’ll have to be careful to always act the part in public, though. You are a good, innocent Catholic school girl raised by a loving grandmother. I’m the good godfather who wants to help and protect you. Understand?”

“Got it.”

CHAPTER 22

His first call was to Margaret. "Good morning, Darling," he crooned. "I need to change my flight and hotel reservations for New York. An extra ticket for Miss Rosalie Alvarez. No, no, not this time," he chuckled. "She's my godchild. Seriously. Her parents died recently and she has no other family, so she's living with me for now. Yes, it's quite a lifestyle change for both of us. At least until she starts college. Seventeen. And change the hotel to a two-room suite and get me two tickets for Saturday night to a musical a young person might enjoy. Whatever. I trust your judgment, as always."

"Who's Margaret?" Rose asked. She strolled into his office wearing one of his dress shirts with the sleeves rolled up. The hem hung down to her knees. He smiled when he saw how cute she looked in his shirt. She smiled, too. He looked so hot with his clinging polo shirt showing off every muscular curve of his chest and arms.

"She's part of the contract I have with my publisher. Since I travel so much and to some unusual locales, I have Margaret always available to take care of all the details. She can arrange any kind of transportation and anything I'll need when I arrive, from theater tickets to native jungle guides, interpreters, visas, you name it. And she knows exactly what I like."

Eric's next call was to the RSVP phone number on the invitation for the awards banquet. "Good morning, Ms. Slade. This is Eric Weber. I would like to add another person to my reservation. Miss Rose Alvarez. No, that's all. Thank you.

"What kind of awards thing is it?"

"A sci-fi writers' organization. Anne Rice is being honored and she invited some other New Orleans writers and friends to attend the banquet."

"You know Anne Rice? I'm so impressed!"

Eric frowned. "Maybe Anne Rice's godchild is impressed that she knows *me*. I'm a famous writer, too, you know."

Rose smiled at him, but didn't acknowledge his obvious request for praise. He already thought too highly of himself. "When do we leave for New York?"

"Tomorrow morning. We'll have a couple of days for shopping and …"

Rose climbed up and straddled Eric in his leather desk chair. She had nothing on underneath the big shirt. "Shopping and what else," she said as she lightly kissed his face all over.

"Whatever you want to do. I want you to have fun in New York," he said caressing her bottom with both of his huge hands. He moaned. Rose felt him grow rock hard under her, pressing against her bare center.

"Eric wants me to have a good time in New York?" His thoughtful concern touched her heart. She wanted to do something nice for him in return. She lifted up on her knees, unzipped his pants and freed his erection. Then she slowly impaled herself

onto him. She grabbed his hair and kissed his mouth as though she could devour him for lunch.

"If she's this impressed that I know Anne Rice, I can't wait to see what she does about Stephen King," he mused.

CHAPTER 23

After they arrived at their hotel in New York City and had lunch, Eric hired a limo and took Rose shopping anywhere she wanted to go. All of the big department stores from Saks Fifth Avenue to Bloomingdale's and every hot little boutique in between. She modeled every outfit for Eric's approval, and he voted thumbs down on anything too short, low-cut or revealing. "You're supposed to be a virtuous young girl," he reminded her often. They shopped in the mornings and went sightseeing in the afternoons.

When Eric told her she had to get an evening gown for the banquet, she frowned at him. "What is this, prom night?" she asked with attitude.

"The invitation said that the requested attire is 'dress to kill,' so I'm wearing a tux and you're wearing a long gown."

"Nothing strapless and everything modestly covered," Eric instructed the clerk who was assisting Rose. She found a fabulous gown that suited Rose's perfect hourglass figure and it wasn't strapless. It was midnight blue and skin tight all the way down. It was cut just low enough to show a little of her breasts bulging out at the top. Rose couldn't believe how beautiful she looked in it. "I'd like to surprise him so I don't want to model it for him," she told the clerk. When Rose rejoined Eric in her street clothes, Eric said he wanted to see the gown *on* her for his approval.

The clerk stepped in. "I'm sorry, Mr. Weber, but the dress has already been sent down to alterations to be hemmed. I can assure you that it meets all your requirements. We will have it delivered to your hotel room in plenty of time."

Rose wore a simple black Diane Von Furstenberg dress and strappy little high heel sandals by Jimmy Choo to dinner and the theater that night to see "Wicked" and felt on top of the world with the whole experience. She did wonder to herself why the theater didn't have popcorn, but didn't mention it to Eric.

On the morning of the banquet, Eric arranged for Rose to have the full glamor treatment at the hotel spa while he met with his publisher. One woman gave her a facial, and two others did her manicure and pedicure. A couple of clients walked by her on their way to get their hair done, both talking lustfully about a man.

"When I saw him in the lobby earlier, I nearly died. He is so *hot*!" the blonde said, fanning herself with her hand.

"I wanted to get his autograph, but my husband threatened to cut up my gold card if I did."

"Who are they talking about? Is there a big movie star in the hotel?" Rose asked the attendants working on her.

"Sweetie, every lady in the hotel is talking about him. Eric Weber, best-selling author, rich international playboy and stud muffin. If you haven't seen him yet, you're in for a treat."

After the spa, Rose returned to the hotel room steamed, massaged, shampooed, styled, toned, exfoliated, moisturized, painted, polished and feeling like a queen.

That night, Eric dressed early and went to the cocktail lounge to meet fellow writers who were staying in the same hotel. They were going to share a limo to the event. Eric told his friends the fake story about his young godchild as they waited for her come down to meet them.

When she walked into the bar, Rose tossed her new cashmere overcoat on a chair so that Eric could see the full effect of her dress. When he saw her, he jumped to his feet in shock. The other two gentlemen stood to greet her also, obviously surprised and pleased. Eric, not so much. He frowned and shook his head, unable to speak.

"You don't like it, Eric? It's not strapless and everything is covered, just like you wanted," she said with as much fake wide-eyed innocence as she could muster. She turned around to show off the gown, her hour glass figure and her gorgeous ass.

"That dress is not appropriate for a girl your age," he said.

"On the contrary. It is absolutely perfect, Ms. Alvarez," gushed one of the gentlemen, taking her hand and escorting her out. Eric grabbed her coat and put it around her as they all left together.

When they returned to the hotel at the end of the evening, hotel staff had iced champagne and a little tray of fresh fruit and sweets waiting for them on a table. An inviting fire in the living room welcomed them in from the cold.

Rose changed into her new silky red lounging dress and joined Eric in the living room. She stretched out on the fuzzy rug by the fire, sipping her champagne. He had shed his shoes, jacket and bow tie and let his shirt hang out comfortably. He was sitting on the sofa. "You looked spectacular tonight," he said softly. "I was afraid that one of those guys would scoop you up and carry you away."

"You were much too intimidating for anyone to try it," she laughed. "Besides, they looked wimpy next to you, standing head and shoulders taller than all of them, looking like a Viking god in that tux. I was the one who should have been worried. All those babes fluttering around you all night. I almost expected them to toss their panties and room keys at you." Eric smiled at the compliment. He was accustomed to that kind of reaction from women, but he was happy that Rose noticed it.

She invited him to join her on the rug. Eric set their glasses aside and lay over her, kissing her neck and shoulders and her willing mouth.

"Take me," she said between kisses.

"To bed?"

"No. *Take* me." Panting with desire, she laid her arms out on the rug, offering herself to him, holding nothing back. "You're a wild savage and I'm your virgin captive," she said, offering him fantasy sex. "You can do anything you want with me. Here, by your campfire."

Like a wild Viking invader, he ripped his dress shirt off, scattering buttons across the room, and with a growl, he ravaged her. She put the back of her hand to her forehead and played along, softly moaning, "Help! Save me!" He was rough, forceful and left light bruises where he held her wrists, but he was exciting, too. His strength left her breathless, with no will to even pretend resistance.

When they were both satisfied, he rolled over on his back and she rolled over on top of him. She stroked his hair and he rubbed her back.

"I gave him the green light to do whatever he wanted. He could have gotten kinky or mean, but he didn't. I can trust him not to hurt me."

With his arms around her, she fell asleep with her head resting on his chest, content and happy, listening to his strong heartbeat.

They woke up two hours later, shared the rest of the champagne and fruit by the fire, and went to bed utterly satisfied.

They slept late the next morning, went sightseeing for the rest of the day and flew back to New Orleans on Monday.

When Rose left New Orleans, her only luggage was her black tote bag with two sets of clothes and the shoes on her feet. When she came back, she had a huge set of new luggage stuffed with designer labels, sexy lingerie, cosmetics and all kinds of shoes and boots.

****

"Eric asked me what I would do if I were rich," she told Jack. "I told him my fantasies about good food, fine clothes, travel to exciting places, and he made all of them come true in New York."

CHAPTER 24

At their next appointment, Eric told Dr. Cushman the whole truth about Rose and their relationship.

"You've spent your whole life running away all over the world, chasing every hedonistic pleasure you could find and coming back home suicidal because nothing took away the anguish. But this girl has changed something. You're gushing like a schoolboy. And you're living together. That's a big step for you."

"It's not a 'step,' it's just a fun arrangement that meets her needs and mine."

"So the two of you aren't falling in love, I take it," Dr. Cushman offered.

"Oh, *hell* no. But this girl is so amazing. She loves sex. Every night. She's insatiable! She even asks me for it in the middle of the day, in the shower, in my office. But except for the great sex, she's a royal pain in the ass. A con artist, stubborn, smart mouth, arrogant, childish ..."

"Well, she *is* a child. Doesn't that bother you?"

Eric didn't get the point of the question, or chose to dodge it. "Yeah. I can't get any work done when she's around. She's so damned distracting."

"What will she do when you don't need her anymore? Will she go back to living on the street when you're gone?"

"She wants to get her GED and start college after that. She wants to stay with me until she graduates. That would be great for me, if she doesn't kill me first," he chuckled.

"You expect you'll be around for at least four years, but after that … she won't be?" Dr. Cushman asked.

"Unless she wants to stay longer."

"Most young women hope to marry and have children eventually, even if they have a successful career."

"She's very young. I doubt she's thought that far ahead," Eric lied. Rose said that was exactly what she wanted.

"She hasn't had the luxury of looking far ahead," Cushman said. "She's had to worry about survival every day. She probably still is."

"Not as long as she's with me. She has everything she wants," Eric countered.

"You're like a life preserver, Eric; but she knows you could kick her out at any time and she would be back living on the street. She's smart enough to realize that without the life preserver, she might sink right back to where she was before."

"I want to take care of her, but I don't want her to hang on to me just because she's desperate and afraid."

"Then stop being a life preserver and teach her to swim."

"What does that mean?"

"Help her to become independent. You know you won't be around to take care of her forever. Maybe not long enough for her to finish school. With you, marriage and children are out of the question. Right now, she's saving you more surely than any doctor can. You could return the favor by saving her from fear and an uncertain future."

"'You can save her and she can save you,' the voice had said." He pondered that in silence. Eric didn't say anything for a while. "How can I do that?"

"She wants to go to college. Maybe you could set up a college fund for her, administered by a third party, to guarantee that no matter what happens between the two of you, her education is secure. With a college education, she could feel confident of employment and never fear becoming homeless again."

"If her education is guaranteed, she might leave me. She wouldn't be saving me after that. I don't want her to be afraid," he said sadly, "but I don't want to lose her either."

"Eric, you have never found peace in running away or any selfish pleasures. Maybe, doing something completely unselfish would give you more than you think. Are you still seeing Dr. Dupuis?"

"Yes. No results yet on the latest drugs, but he's hopeful."

CHAPTER 25

The weather in early December was mostly dry and pleasant. New Orleans was ending another year with no hurricanes, no major rain storms and no flooding. The economy was healthy, the years of rebuilding after Hurricane Katrina brought jobs and hope, and the city was celebrating the season with parties, music and extravagant decorations.

Eric received stacks of invitations to dinners and parties, but was reluctant to go. He didn't want to leave Rose at home alone or ask someone else to be his date or bring a teenager to an adult gathering. It was less complicated to just stay home.

"People will start to wonder why the famous international playboy has become a hermit," Rose said. "You should get a date and go to these things. You've been seen all around town with me, but for these adult-only events, you need to have an older woman on your arm. And, when friends ask you to join them for happy hour or lunch or a game of golf, you should go."

"Should I sleep with these ladies? You know, just to keep up my image?" he teased.

"I told you before that monogamy was not part of our agreement. It's up to you. If you don't mind second best," she smirked.

Eric took her suggestion and went back to normal socializing, occasionally with a date, but mostly going out alone to meet friends. One party invitation was to the gated neighborhood of Audubon Place, off St. Charles Avenue. To buy a house there, you had to have a ton of money, but more than that, you had to have the right pedigree and social connections. It was a black tie affair, of course. The hostess suggested that Eric bring Rose with him, because her college aged children, who were home for the holidays, would be there to keep her company.

Eric brought a date, a fashion model named Inga with the tall skinny body of a boy. No boobs, hips or butt, but lots of eye makeup and arrogance. He did his best to avoid looking at Rose during the party for two reasons. First, in a black velvet party dress, she looked good enough to eat and he didn't want his date to think she was the reason for his body heat. Second, it made him crazy the way Rose flirted so outrageously with the college boys, laughed at their jokes and ignored her "godfather" completely.

Inga noticed how he kept an eye on Rose. "It's sweet that you're so concerned about the child, Darling, but none of those boys will try get in her panties while you're here. Relax and dance with me."

Eric made a point of ignoring Rose after that, and showering his own date with attention, flattery and seductive teasing. After the party, Eric drove Rose home first, then left with Inga. He wanted Rose to be jealous.

Rose waited up for him. By two a.m. she was having trouble staying awake, so she sat on the stairs to wait. If she did fall asleep, she would hear him come in and wake up.

Eric smiled when he saw her asleep on the stairs, still wearing her party dress. She woke up when he sat down beside her and stretched out his long legs down the stairs.

"Where have you been for so late?" Rose asked with a yawn.

He leaned back with his elbows on the stairs, happy that she was concerned. "It's none of your business," he said, undoing his tie and unbuttoning his collar, "but Inga had tickets for Tipitina's show tonight. Wynton Marsalis was there so we talked for a while. Then Inga and I went out for a late supper."

"Did you do the skinny girl?"

"No," he said. "I've known Inga a long time. She's second best." He smiled at Rose and pulled her face close to his.

Rose believed him, mostly; but monogamy wasn't part of their agreement. Eric never was the type to pass up sex with a beautiful woman. Second best was still not bad.

She got up, took his hand and led him upstairs to his bedroom to show him again what first best was like.

CHAPTER 26

Evelyn loved to cook for Rose, frequently introducing her palate to new tastes. Rose could never afford to be a picky eater, and she enjoyed everything put on the table. Evelyn made Eggs Neptune for breakfast, a southern variation of Eggs Benedict with a generous helping of lump crabmeat replacing the Canadian bacon. Rose savored it slowly.

"Eric, its December. Let's go get our Christmas tree today," Rose asked.

"We won't be here for Christmas, Rosie," Eric said without looking up from his newspaper.

"Why not?"

"Our passports have arrived and we're going to spend Christmas week in Cozumel, lying on a white sand beach, swimming in water as warm and clear as bathwater and coming back home with a tan. I can hardly wait."

"Couldn't we go there before Christmas week? I've never had a Christmas tree in my whole life. Please, Eric."

"A kid who never had a tree? I can't refuse her a simple Christmas tree."

"Okay. I'll move up our trip and you can have a tree."

Eric called Margaret to change his trip reservations. "Any date, as long as we're back home by Christmas week," he told her.

Margaret called back later in the day. "I can get you there on the fourteenth and back home on the twentieth. Will that work for you?" Rose saw what Eric marked on his desk calendar and answered for him. "Perfect, Margaret! Thank you!" she shouted at the phone. Margaret laughed.

"I'll have Otis get you a tree in his pick-up and set it up in the family room. You and Evelyn can go shopping for tree lights and ornaments."

Since all of the rooms in the old mansion had high ceilings, Rose told Otis to get a tree ten feet tall. He brought in a ladder and helped them decorate the top. She had her first Christmas tree up and decorated the following day, and sat in the family room every night enjoying the wonder of it while she listened to holiday music on the radio.

Eric told Rose to pack only one carry-on bag with casual clothes and sandals for their trip. They could buy swimsuits and anything else they needed when they got there. Rose was delighted to hear it. No evening gowns and unlimited shopping for fun clothes!

The day they left for the airport to go to Cozumel, it was cold and drizzling in New Orleans, the temperature just above freezing. Evelyn followed them out to the taxi to retrieve their umbrellas before they drove off, and waved them goodbye from the curb.

Rose thought about the homeless people out in weather like this and shivered, remembering it too well. One bitterly cold rainy Christmas Eve was spent sleeping on a pew in the chapel of Veteran's Hospital. There were so few patients and staff in the hospital on a holiday that she slept undisturbed all night. It wasn't cushy, but it was peaceful, warm and dry. You could find all kinds of places like that if you got creative and thought outside the box. Even if somebody caught you where you shouldn't be, you might be left alone if you were nicely dressed and didn't look like a trespassing bum.

She and Eric were bundled up in layers, so they could shed what wasn't needed as they went to warmer latitudes. When they arrived in Mexico, the weather was perfect. Warm and breezy under clear bright blue skies. They stuffed their sweaters and long sleeved shirts in their carry-on bags before leaving the airport terminal and enjoyed the warm sun on their faces.

"Let's go shopping for swimsuits and go the beach this afternoon," Rose said. Eric wanted to take her to bed first, but he gave in to her easily, as usual.

They caught a taxi from the hotel to the tourist shops. Rose was as excited as a child at Disneyland. "Can I get whatever I want?" she asked Eric.

"Here," he said, handing her two $100 bills. "I'm going to buy my swimsuit, then head over to that little bar across the street to wait for you and have a drink. Join me when you get finished."

Rose squealed and hugged him around his ribs. She bought a wide brim straw hat, a big straw tote bag, two beach towels, a string bikini, sunscreen lotion, a couple of tee shirts, denim shorts, sunglasses and a halter top sundress. When she ran out of cash, she put on her straw hat and sunglasses and joined Eric at the bar.

Eric watched her bounce across the street and appreciated how young and energetic she was. God, he wanted her so *bad*! She babbled on about the cute things she had in the armload of bags, but Eric couldn't hear a thing she said. Her enthusiasm turned him on and all he could think about was going back to their hotel room for an "afternoon delight."

His need was urgent, but Rose had an urgent need of her own. She had never owned a swimsuit, never walked on a beach and never saw clear ocean water. While Eric was in the bathroom shaving, Rose pulled on shorts and a tee shirt over her bikini, stuffed the rest of her beach gear in her straw beach bag and headed for the door.

"Hurry up, Eric!" she called to him. "I'm ready and I'll wait for you in the lobby!" She was out the door before Eric could answer her.

He slumped against the bathroom counter with his arms folded, feeling cheated. Then his face brightened with a wonderful thought. Sex on the beach! "Not just a good cocktail, but a good afternoon," he said to himself in the mirror. While he finished shaving, he fantasized about untying her string bikini with his teeth. He pulled on his shirt and raced to the lobby to meet Rose.

The bartender he spoke to earlier while waiting for Rose to do her shopping told him about a little cove a few miles from town that wasn't visible from the road. When the tide goes out, a wide strip of sandy beach was revealed. The water was shallow for a long way out, so the waves broke a good distance from the shore.

"It's quiet and private," the bartender said. "If you want to try it, the tide is out this afternoon and won't come back until after dark." He told Eric how to find it. "When you're ready to come back to the hotel, just climb back up the rocky trail to the top and wait by the road for the next bus to come by. Wave at him and he'll stop for you."

Eric and Rose took a taxi out of town and stopped on the road at the spot described by the bartender. They made their way down the rocky path slowly to their own private little beach.

Rose took off her shorts and shirt and splashed around the edge of the water. Eric ran way out where the water was deep enough to swim. "Come out here and swim with me," he called to her.

"I can't swim! You go. I'm happy right here." She lay on her back with her arms spread out in the foot-deep water close to the beach, grinning and splashing gently with her hands and feet. Tiny fish swam close to her and she shooed them away with a giggle. Eric came back in to the water's edge and stretched out in the warm shallow water beside her.

"I felt an odd sense of safety in that little cove," she told Jack. "The world and its dangers were out there somewhere, but we were sheltered in the cove by the cliffs on three sides and the calm water. Nobody there to bother us. When I was about six or seven, I went outside during the night. I always left the house when my parents were having a knock down drag out fight. I didn't want to become collateral damage, so I'd usually sit on the back steps until they quit. In winter cold or summer mosquitos, I'd sit on those steps in the dark, sometimes for hours. I was always afraid out there. Sometimes a stray dog would come around and growl at me. I heard noises in the yard and I thought a monster might get me. When I went back to my bed I had trouble falling asleep again. A big, noisy storm with lightning and thunder was blowing through one time and I had wrapped an old blanket around myself. I couldn't stay outside in the rain, so I got in the neighbor's unlocked car. The bad stuff was out there, but inside the car, wrapped in a blanket, it felt cozy. Safe and protected. On that little beach with Eric, that's how it felt to me. It was strange."

The water was a brilliant blue-green and still. Waves broke a long way out, but the sound echoed softly against the rock cliffs behind them. It was a soothing, romantic sound.

The little bikini Rose wore was nothing but three triangles of cloth, covering only enough to be legal. Eric thought about tossing his swimsuit on the beach and doing it with Rose there in the shallow water.

Before he could act on that impulse, four teenagers came down the trail from the top of the cliff to the beach. They were laughing and shouting to each other, struggling to descend the trail with their ice chest, towels and beach bags. Eric stood up and moved away from Rose. When the kids got down to the sand, one of the boys recognized Eric and excitedly came over to greet him and report that he was a big fan.

"Oh, man!" the boy exclaimed. "My friends will not believe that I actually met Eric Weber in person! Would you mind taking a photograph with us?"

Eric charmingly agreed, as always. He could never disappoint a fan. The teenagers went swimming and Eric sat in the sand on a beach towel away from Rose.

"That was close. What was I thinking? Sex on the beach? Those kids with a smart phone could have splashed a picture of my naked butt on the internet and the cover of every tabloid in the country. My publisher would drop me like a hot rock."

CHAPTER 27

The following days on the island were spent like any other tourists'. Eating, drinking, getting a tan and sightseeing. Eric rented one of the yellow mopeds seen all over the island and they went exploring. Rose rode behind him, holding on tight and laughing wildly at his fearless driving. They spent a day at Paradise Beach eating gourmet food and wading in the shallow end of the beach. Eric swam laps in the gigantic swimming pool while Rose worked on her tan in the sun.

Back in town, Rose persuaded Eric to go to a popular dance club where young people hung out at night to drink, dance and enjoy their kind of loud music. The club had a live band that night, playing both Caribbean and Spanish rock tunes.

Eric wouldn't dance to rock music, but when he left Rose alone at the table and went to the bar, a young man asked her to dance to a song that had a hot salsa rhythm to it. Rose tossed her long hair and moved her hips and shoulders in ways that burned up the floor. As long as she appeared to be dateless, other young men continuously asked her to dance.

When one young guy put his hands on Rose's behind, Eric was ready to grab him and sling him from the nearest window. An older American man at the bar grabbed Eric's arm to stop him.

"Let her go, Pops. The young people are just having fun. Those boys won't do anything serious as long as her father is keeping an eye on her."

"Father, my ass!" he thought to himself, offended. *"I could have every woman in this bar."* Eric stayed at the bar sulking and let her have her fun. He watched her turn on every guy in the room, including himself. When they got back to their hotel suite, Eric felt like he had to prove his prowess, and took Rose with such fierce passion he was like a man fresh out of prison.

When they were done, Rose felt like she had been hit by a tornado. "Goodness, Eric! What brought that on? You were like a wild man!"

"You bring out the beast in me," he said with a little growl, pulling her tight against his chest.

On their last day in Cozumel, while Rose was shopping for a gift for Evelyn, Eric was again recognized on the street by a couple of fans, Doug and Dottie Palko. They were Americans, thirtyish, expensively dressed and well-educated. They came to Cozumel on their own sailboat almost every winter. Eric did some sailing in the South Seas years ago for a book he was writing, and knew he had met fellow adventurers like himself. He liked them right away.

"Come sail with us around the island this afternoon," Doug offered. "We like to drop anchor near one of the restaurants on the beaches and swim to shore for lunch. It's a lot of fun."

"Sounds great! Do you have a life jacket on board? Rose doesn't know how to swim."

"We have a bin full of 'em," Doug assured him. "Enough for a crowd, if needed."

Eric told Rose about the Palkos' invitation, but failed to mention that they were going to jump off the boat and swim to lunch. He was afraid she would refuse to go, but believed that she would enjoy it as long as she knew that both he and the life jacket would keep her safe.

Rose loved the sailboat and asked Captain Doug to show her how to man the sails. She learned fast and was having a great time.

"Prepare to come about," Doug called to Rose.

"Aye aye, Captain," she said as she went to the bow.

"Release the jib, Matey."

She untied the sail and pulled the rope to the other side of the boat in a smooth motion, like a pro.

"Ready about!" he called out to her. She ducked as the main sail swung above her head, then pulled the jib in tight and tied it off properly. The sailboat made a smooth ninety degree turn. Doug, Dottie and Eric applauded.

"Well done, Sailor," they all said. Rose was grinning with pride.

When they got to the leeward side of the island, where the water was calm and clear, Doug dropped the anchor as close to shore as possible. It was a short swim of a few yards to shallow water and the beach.

"This is San Francisco Beach," Doug said. "The food and drinks here are the best on the island! Let's go get 'em!" Doug and Dottie took off their cover shirts and dove overboard.

"Come on. We're going, too." Eric said to Rose.

"No no no no, Eric. Not me," she protested.

"You have on a life jacket. You can't drown. I will be with you in the water. You'll be fine, I promise," he said as reassuringly as he could. "I won't let anything happen to you."

Eric picked her up in his arms and jumped overboard feet first. Rose screamed like she was being tossed to sharks. Eric held her close to his chest and slowly paddled both of them to shore. She clung to Eric's neck for dear life, crying hysterically the whole time.

When they got to the beach, Eric removed Rose's life jacket and held her close until she calmed down and stopped crying. Doug and Dottie were already in the open-air restaurant, drinking out of coconuts and waiting to eat. "Poor child," Dottie said. "Are you going to be alright?"

"I've never been in anything deeper than a bathtub," she said. "I was terrified."

"I'm so sorry, Rose," Eric kept saying over and over. "I didn't know how afraid you would be. When we get home, you're going to take swimming lessons."

"Dr. Cushman was right in more ways than one. Stop being her life preserver. Teach her to swim."

A powerboat driver offered to take Rose and Eric back to the sailboat when they were ready to go after lunch. Dottie manned the sails on the way back to the city and the rest of the day on the water was fine.

Rose went straight to bed in the late afternoon, exhausted by her ordeal and the long day in the sun. Eric got a text message on his phone that made him want to throw the damned thing off the third floor balcony. An appointment with Dr.

Dupuis when he got home. It had to be bad news. If he had good news, Dupuis would have phoned.

He paced around the hotel room, despondent and angry. While Rose slept, he went to the hotel's outdoor bar to get stinking drunk. The bar jutted out onto the beach, on a sheltered patio surrounded by tall palm trees swaying in the light breeze. The soft whoosh of the surf accompanied a steel drum band playing dance music for vacationing or honey-mooning couples. Soft lights and dreamily romantic atmosphere only accentuated the loneliness of singles who hadn't yet found The One this Christmas. Women gravitated to the handsome stranger at the bar, but Eric ignored them. He wasn't looking for what they offered.

He was looking for hope, or at least enough alcohol to keep him from looking into the bottomless pit. He was feeling mad as hell at the world for his lousy luck. When it got dark, he staggered back to the hotel room and passed out on the couch.

CHAPTER 28

Rose woke him up in the morning. "We're leaving today, remember? I have everything packed except a change of clothes for you. Go take your shower. It's getting late."

"Why'd he sleep on the couch last night? Did he pick up a girl at the bar? Is he bored with me? I ruined the trip for him on the sailboat. He came here to party and I embarrassed him by getting hysterical. He wouldn't even sleep in the same bed with me. He's gonna want me to leave."

They hardly spoke on the flight from Mexico to Atlanta, and from Atlanta to New Orleans. Only what was necessary. The taxi ride home was silent, too. Despite her youth, Rose already understood one important thing about men. They don't talk about their feelings. Asking him what was wrong would only aggravate him further. If he wanted her to leave, she didn't want to hear it anyway.

Evelyn had all of the house lights on to welcome them home, and had fresh baked Christmas cookies in the kitchen. The Christmas tree lights were on. She had a pot of jambalaya ready, if they were hungry.

"Uh-oh, something's wrong," Evelyn thought to herself, noticing that they barely looked at each other. "They're acting like they came back from a funeral, not a tropical vacation."

They each ate a little in silence, then went their separate ways. Eric played pool by himself, drowning the demons in a fresh bottle of bourbon. Rose went upstairs to watch television in bed and to wait up for Eric.

Eric came to the bedroom about midnight, drunk and feeling rejected because she was asleep and not concerned about him. Her message was even clearer when he found her wearing blue flannel pajamas instead of sleeping nude as they always did.

The only message intended by the warm pajamas was that the bed was cold without Eric's body heat next to her. She woke up when he roughly removed her pajama bottoms and he was inside of her before she could even say anything. Neither of them spoke. Eric satisfied himself quickly and fell asleep on top of Rose when he was done.

"Wham, bam, thank you ma'am. All he had to do was wake me up. He didn't need to act like that. Maybe he's trying to drive me away." She shed a few tears, then rolled him over and went back to sleep.

Rose left the house in the morning after having breakfast alone, while Eric slept off his bourbon. She went for a long walk along St. Charles Avenue to think and get in a better mood before he woke up. Cold wet weather had moved on while they were in Mexico. Skies were clear and bright and it was a perfect 50 degrees.

It was four days until Christmas. Holiday decorations festooned every house and lamp post along the way. Even the streetcars were decorated with garlands and fake frost sprayed in the windows. But Rose wasn't feeling the joy that she expected now that she was living in a real home with a real Christmas tree, like normal people. She wasn't alone or on the outside looking in anymore. What she felt was fear. Fear that Eric wanted her to leave.

She stopped walking a few blocks from home. "I don't know what's bothering him. Maybe it's me, maybe it's something else he doesn't want to talk about. But I'm not going to give up on him. I'm going to be extra sweet to him and get him out of his mood. I'll apologize for ruining his trip." At the spot where she stopped, a black and white Tuxedo kitten ran out from under a hedge and back in again. She laughed at it and tried to call it back out. The gardener, who was outside cleaning up the front yard, heard her.

"Would you like to adopt a kitten, Miss?" he asked politely, coming out around the hedge to speak to her on the sidewalk. "A stray cat had a litter of 'em under the front porch. I've been feedin' 'em and they're pretty tame." He picked up the one that was playing under the hedge and offered it to her. Rose accepted the tiny fur ball and cuddled it to her face.

"Oh, she's precious! I'll take her. Thank you." Rose turned around and slowly walked back home, petting and talking baby talk to her first pet.

When Rose returned, Evelyn was loading her car with wrapped Christmas presents and suitcases to spend the holiday with her daughter and grandchildren in Baton Rouge. She didn't usually leave town because Eric had so many holiday parties from Christmas to New Year's, so her family came to New Orleans to visit with her instead. Eric invited them to his parties when they were in town. But none were planned this year. Evelyn thought Eric was troubled about something, but didn't ask why.

Evelyn was delighted with Rose's new kitten and welcomed it to the house. She opened a can of tuna for her and served it on a china plate. "I have to go back to the store for a few things I forgot before I leave, so I'll add cat food and litter to the list," she said. "I made up a few casseroles and other things for you to eat while I'm gone. Eat the ones in the fridge first so they don't spoil and the rest are in the freezer."

Evelyn returned from the store, put away the groceries and said her goodbye to Rose. Rose hugged Evelyn and wished her a safe trip.

Rose carried her little kitten around with her throughout the house. Eric came downstairs around two in the afternoon, showered, shaved and casually dressed in jeans and a dark blue sweater. He looked like he was still upset about something.

"Are you hungry?"

"I'll grab something downtown. I have some business to take care of." He was in a dark mood and went for his overcoat without even looking at Rose.

"I'll heat Evelyn's casserole for supper, if you want."

"I don't know," he mumbled. He turned to leave and saw the kitten she was holding. "Where did you get that?" he asked curtly, glaring at both of them.

"She's a stray I found when I went for a walk this morning. I named her Precious."

"Keep it outside. I don't want that thing in the house." Eric went out the back door to the garage and left in his car.

"We're not going to give up on him, are we, Precious? He'll be okay. And I'm not going to put you outside in the cold."

"I really do need some good news today. I don't know how much longer my mind can take it," he thought. Eric went into the office building downtown and came out ninety minutes later. The news he got weighed heavily on his shoulders. Christmas music drifted out to the sidewalk from an electronics store nearby. People with loaded shopping bags rushed along, smiling and wishing others a Merry Christmas. Eric couldn't manage a smile or a response. He wanted to run away, somewhere else in the world, like he always had in the past. Instead, he went to Molly's.

CHAPTER 29

Molly's on Decatur Street is a grungy little bar that suited his mood for the day. He hung out there a lot in his younger days, drinking lightly and people-watching. Interesting or oddball customers he met there often ended up in his books. Mr. Wu, the resident cat owned by one of the upstairs tenants, walked down the bar to greet the familiar face. "Go away, Wu. I'm not in the mood for conversation," Eric said. Mr. Wu went to find a more jovial patron further down the bar.

"Whatcha got cold, Walter?" he asked the bartender, a red-haired Scotsman with a bushy mustache.

A man sitting on the barstool next to him said with a laugh, "If you want something cold, order the coffee. If you want something warm, order the beer." Walter the bartender pretended to be irate with the guy, but it was friendly teasing from a regular customer.

Eric ordered bourbon on the rocks. He noticed an unconscious middle-aged man sitting on the floor in a corner, leaning against the wall and snoring loudly. He had only one shoe. Nobody seemed to be concerned about the fellow, though.

"What's with him?" Eric asked the bartender.

"He's okay. He gave me the phone number of his chauffeur when he came in. The limo is on its way."

"He has his own limo and a driver?? He looks like a filthy derelict."

"Yeah, but he's a rich businessman. Rents big equipment to the oil drilling companies. He becomes a drunken bum a couple times a year, dragging through the Quarter for a few days until he can't stand up any more. Then his driver scoops him up and takes him home," he explained nonchalantly. In the French Quarter, nobody thought that was strange.

****

Rose had an early supper, then took Precious upstairs for a bath with the flea shampoo Evelyn brought home. Warm water and Rose's gentle massage were soothing and the kitten didn't put up a struggle. When Precious was dry, Rose took a shower and put on her red lounging dress. It brought back a sexy memory of New York, and she hoped it would improve Eric's mood when he got home.

She lit a fire in the family room fireplace and curled up on the sofa with her kitten to watch Christmas specials on television until Eric came home. Precious wasn't allowed in the family room since the Christmas tree went up, but she was content to cuddle with Rose and leave the tree unmolested for once.

Rose wasn't going to go to bed without Eric this time, no matter how late he came home.

Eric came in at ten o'clock. "Would you like to come in the family room and sit by the fire with me for a while?" Rose asked gently. Eric looked like hell and smelled of alcohol.

"No, it's late and I'm tired. Come to bed," he growled as he headed up the stairs.

Rose didn't follow him, but stood at the bottom of the stairs, looking at him with confusion and sympathy. She wanted to comfort him and make his bad mood go away. "What are you so upset about, Eric? Talk to me."

Eric stopped and turned to look at Rose. She wasn't coming upstairs and she still had the stray cat. "I told you I didn't want that cat in the house. Put it outside and come to bed," he commanded in a loud and angry voice.

Rose was shocked. "No. This is the first pet I've ever had and I love her. I can't put her outside, all alone in the cold and the dark," Rose said calmly. "We need each other."

Eric came back down and stopped on the bottom stair, so that he towered above Rose even more than usual. He leaned down toward her and said in a tone that sounded threatening, "If you want a pet we can get something that is at least clean and pure bred. I will not have a dirty stray cat off the street in my house! Now put it outside and come to bed *now*." It was an angry order, not a request.

Rose felt like she had been slapped in the face. "That's what he called me, once … a stray cat off the street. That's what he still thinks of me. That's why he's been so upset lately. He doesn't want me here anymore."

"No," she said to him again with tears running down her face. "I'm not getting rid of my kitten and I'm not coming to bed with you until you calm down and we can discuss this."

"We have an agreement, Rose," he shouted. "I have every right to expect you in my bed every night."

"Let's go sit in the family room, because we're renegotiating that agreement right here and right now!"

He came downstairs and picked her up around the waist with one arm. He was going to carry her upstairs to bed and force himself on her, like her uncle did. Rose went ballistic.

"No you won't!" Screaming at him, she kicked him in the shins and bit his hand as hard as she could to free herself. She ran into the family room and he came after her, furious, sucking on his bleeding hand. She crossed her arms defiantly.

He grabbed the front of her gown and raised his hand to slap her hard across her mouth for biting him, but he knew from experience in more than one barroom brawl that he might break her jaw or knock out a few teeth. So he released her and clenched his fists at his side.

"I don't need this from you, Rose. I'm going out of my mind! If you're going to defy me, break our agreement and bite me like some damned alley cat, then get out!" He waved his arm in a sweeping motion and shouted at the ceiling, "Get out of my house! Out of my *life*! And take your damned cat with you!" he roared.

"Fine! We're leaving!" she yelled back at him. "I was right all along. He was tired of me and wanted me out. The cat is just an excuse."

Rose should have remembered an important lesson from growing up with a violent and drunken father. When an angry man tells you to get out, then just get out. Don't push your luck. But Rose was still a child, too young and too hurt to think rationally about cause and effect at that moment.

She grabbed a crystal vase on the way out of the room and hurled it at the big screen TV, shattering both.

Before she could stomp out of the room, Eric grabbed her arm. Everything he was dealing with at that moment overwhelmed him. He was mad at God and the world and Rose, but he took it all out on Rose, simply because she was within reach.

"Enough of this, little girl," he growled in a low voice. He grabbed the back of her hair in his big fist and pushed her toward the nearest chair, holding her at arm's length to keep her from kicking or biting him again.

"Ow, ow, ow," she screeched, trying to get her hair out of his grip. She kicked over a table and shattered a lamp.

He sat down and roughly shoved her face down across his lap. "NO! Eric, stop! We have an agreement! You said you would never hit me!" she pleaded, flailing arms and legs to get away.

"As you said, Rose, we're renegotiating our agreement, right *here* and right *now*!" She screamed and fought with all her might, but Eric's size and strength were more than enough to hold her in place without much effort. He pushed her gown up and pulled her panties down, then wacked her bare behind over and over until his rage was spent and he came to his senses.

His hand was still in mid-air, ready to strike again, when he saw that Rose wasn't struggling anymore. She was limp and sobbing deeply, barely able to catch her breath. He held her where she was, shocked at how red her skin was and how much he hurt her.

Eric was trembling. He carefully pulled up her panties and lifted her to her feet. He wanted to hold her in his arms and beg for forgiveness, but he was afraid for her. He was out of his mind. She needed to get away from him or he might hurt her again.

Too overcome for her legs to hold her up, she crumpled to the floor in front of him, still sobbing uncontrollably. Not just from the burning of her skin, but from a broken heart. A few days before Christmas, and she was abused, unwanted and homeless again.

Rose always knew that Eric could ask her to leave at any time, but she didn't think that he actually would. Life with Eric had been safe, comfortable and exciting. And sex with Eric was the best ever. She didn't want to believe that Eric could be like every other man. He said once, when the time came, they would part as friends, not like this.

"Sleep in your own room. Pack your things and clear out in the morning," Eric said calmly.

He numbly dragged himself to his office, hating himself. The tiny kitten trotted behind him and climbed up the upholstery of his big armchair to sit on his lap. Eric was staring vacantly into space and didn't notice. Precious tapped him on the chest with her little white paw and meowed to get his attention. Without thinking, Eric petted the cat until she curled up in the crook of his arm and went to sleep, purring.

An hour later, he brought the kitten to Rose's bedroom and closed the door to keep it there, then went to his bedroom alone. He didn't sleep all night. The despair was so deep, he thought about loading his pistol and ending it all. Why hang on? His pain had now hurt someone else.

Rose continued sobbing on the floor of the family room for hours. Her grief was so deep she couldn't bear it either. There was no one in the world who cared for her. No place to call home. "I'm not strong anymore, Grandma," she whispered out loud. "I don't want to live like this. I'd rather die than spend the rest of my life alone. What am I going to do?" She stopped crying and tried to think.

She had some money saved for school and could use it to get a cheap hotel room until she could find an apartment somewhere. No point in trying to find a job during the holidays. Businesses were closed or the extra holiday employees were already on the job. When the fire in the family room burned itself out, Rose got up from the cold floor and went to her own bedroom to wash her face, pack a few things and decide where to go from there.

"Just barely a month. It didn't take him long." Shutting off her emotions as best she could, she prepared herself to face life alone again. "Okay. Get hold of yourself and stop crying. At least my situation is not as bad as it was. I have cash savings, nice clothes and what I need now to get a job. I can make it. I don't care what happens to me." She double-checked to make sure she packed her Social Security card, birth certificate and passport in her suitcase.

She changed into her favorite jeans and a pair of long brown leather boots, topping it off with a turtleneck sweater and her cashmere overcoat. She planned to let Eric cool down before returning for the rest of her things.

At sunrise, Eric heard Rose leave out of the front door, setting off the burglar alarm. From his bedroom window, he saw her walking toward downtown, with only her smallest suitcase and a small designer shoulder purse. Precious was tucked inside her coat. By the time he got downstairs, she was getting on the street car and riding away, disappearing in the thick early morning fog.

He hadn't thought about what he would say to her if he had gotten to her in time. Would he apologize and beg her to stay? No. She needed to get away from him and anybody else who would mistreat her.

That was what *she* needed. What *he* needed was … what? A drink? A miracle? He hated to admit it, but he needed … *her*. He needed her to keep him sane. The peace that her body gave him when they were together. Her joy that kept his spirits up. Even her stubbornness. She wasn't really an aggravation, she was just being a kid.

Eric looked in the family room at the Christmas tree that was still lit up from the night before, and at the damages in the room from their fight. *"She was a kid who never even had a Christmas tree, and I spoiled her and gave her everything she wanted and more. I taught her to expect everything. Everything except that little cat. So she threw a temper tantrum. How could I let this happen?"*

He looked in her room and found almost all of her things still there, untouched. She left her last weekly salary of $500 in cash on the dresser with a note. "For the damages."

He slumped down on her bed. "FUCK!" he shouted in regret. "I've never hit a woman in my life. I'm losing my mind. Why didn't I just let her keep the cat?"

****

Rose didn't tell Jack all the details about the fight, only that Eric didn't want the cat in the house and she refused to put it outside. "I identified with my kitten, a defenseless little thing out in the cold and dark, like I had been. I couldn't do it. I had a desperate need to protect her because nobody protected me. So Precious and I left in the morning."

CHAPTER 30

Steven and Gary had a lovely, spacious apartment in a historic old building. Like most of the other high-priced rentals in the Quarter, it had large rooms, high ceilings, original hardwood floors and doors that opened onto a balcony with a beautiful wrought iron railing. Gary, a successful art gallery owner, had impeccable taste in decorating the place. When Rose left Eric's house, she went to see them first. Steven's sister Noreen was visiting him when Rose arrived.

"Hey, Rose! What a surprise! Merry Christmas!" Steven said. "Come in! Where have you been? We haven't seen you around lately."

"I've been staying at my godfather's house since Thanksgiving, but we had a big fight and he put me out. You and Gary are the only friends I have, and I was hoping that you might offer me some clues about looking for work and locating an apartment. I have some money to hold me for a while, but I've never done this before and I don't know where to start."

Steven's sister Noreen offered to help. She and her family had a two-hundred-year-old Greek revival two-story townhouse on Esplanade at the edge of the Quarter. The brick-walled courtyard at the back of the house had a little efficiency apartment that would be available for Rose to rent after the holidays. It was originally built as the outdoor kitchen building where slaves did the cooking. When the main house had a modern kitchen added inside, the empty building was converted into living quarters for hired servants. About thirty years ago, when the owners could no longer afford full-time servants, the little building was renovated and upgraded to a one-bedroom rental unit. Until the unit was vacated, Rose was invited to stay with Steven and Gary and sleep on their sofa.

"We have a cat, too," Gary said, "So yours is welcome here. Aren't you, Precious?" he said to the kitten. "What's her name?"

"Precious," Rose said, and everyone laughed.

Steven's sister graciously offered to drive Rose back to her godfather's house to collect the rest of her things, but Rose declined.

"We parted on bad terms and I'm afraid I'd break down and cry if I went back and saw him again. I really liked staying with him. We weren't blood relatives, but he was the closest thing to it."

"Well then, I could go and get your things by myself, if you think he'd let me take them. Actually, he might even prefer it that way, to avoid any unpleasantness. I won't be able to do it until after New Year's, though, because I have a house full of family and guests for the holidays. Can you get along with what you have with you for a week?"

Rose assured her that she would be fine, and thanked her profusely for her kindness.

Noreen Odom felt sad for the girl to be homeless for Christmas, and invited her to Christmas dinner at her house.

"No need, Sis," Steven said. "Gary and I are having a big gang of friends over for Christmas dinner and Rose will enjoy herself right here."

"Thanks, all of you," Rose said with a smile. She wrote down the name and address of her godfather for Ms. Odom before she went back to her own home. "I really appreciate your doing this for me."

Noreen Odom was shocked when she looked at the note. "Your godfather is Eric Weber? *The* Eric Weber, the writer?"

Rose nodded.

"I can't imagine a famous man like that turning his back on a homeless godchild. What is the world coming to? Umm, umm, umm," she said shaking her head.

"To be fair," Rose said, "he's a lifelong bachelor and having me around was a huge change for him. It was stressful, I guess. The argument was my fault."

CHAPTER 31

Steven and Gary had a huge Christmas dinner with a houseful of friends," she told Jack. "They were all like me, with no family to spend the holiday with. Everybody brought something to add to the party. Evelyn told me what happened when Ms. Odom came here a week later to get my things. I was afraid that Eric was still mad and he would slam the door in her face, but he didn't."

****

Eric looked like hell when he answered the door bell. He hadn't been sleeping well since Rose left. The bed felt cold and empty. He drank too much and he hadn't shaved in two days. He had run his hands through his hair in frustration so many times it stood out from his scalp, looking like a bad Mohawk. He was still wearing his workout clothes from that morning.

"Hello, Mr. Weber," the middle-aged lady visitor at the front door said. She was nicely dressed and as cheerful as an Avon Lady. "My name is Noreen Odom. I'm a friend of Ms. Alvarez."

"Is Ms. Alvarez alright?" he asked anxiously.

"Oh, yes, she's just fine," she said cheerily. "She sent me to ask you if it would be okay for me to get the things she left here. I can put them in my car."

"She didn't want to come in person because she's afraid of me," he thought. *"Or she hates me."*

"Tomorrow would be better, Ms. Odom. I'll get everything packed and have it ready for you. By the way, Ms. Alvarez didn't say where she would be staying when she left. Is she with you?"

"No. She's staying at my brother's house. It's a beautiful place, lots of room. She's comfortable there and Steven likes cats." She didn't mention that her brother was the gay fashionista Rose already knew. If Mr. Weber thought his godchild was forced to live in sin with a strange man, and it was his fault for kicking the child out on the street … well, good. She thought the rat bastard should feel guilty.

"Well then, I'll see you about ten o'clock tomorrow?"

"Yes. Ten is fine. Goodbye." Noreen thought that Rose would be pleased to know that Eric looked even more miserable than she was.

Evelyn overheard the conversation at the door. When she returned from Baton Rouge after Christmas, Rose was already gone, and Eric didn't want to talk about it. She sensed that something was wrong when they returned from Cozumel, and she was right. After Ms. Odom left, Eric followed Evelyn to the kitchen for a cup of coffee.

"Are you going to ask Rose to come back?"

"No," he said. "I can't save her."

Evelyn frowned at him, thinking that was an odd answer. "Save her? I was thinking she could save *you*."

Eric felt like the floor had dropped out from under him. He sat down to keep from spilling his coffee. The voice had said he could save Rose and she could save him. Dr. Cushman said the same thing. Now Evelyn.

"Why would she come back? I hurt her and threw her out. She has a new man already. Steven. Maybe he's good to her. Or maybe he's just a handy schmuck with nothing to offer. The best thing I can offer her now is a chance to find a nice guy. Steven or whoever." Eric continued to mull it over for the rest of the day. "Maybe … maybe she would come back, if ... what? What can I give her that she wants and needs the most? Could she forgive me?" Then Dr. Cushman's advice came back to him.

With a sense of hope, Eric personally folded and packed all of Rose's clothes carefully in her set of luggage and put them near the front door. He wrapped and packed her toiletries and makeup separately in her straw beach bag and put it with the suitcases. In the suitcase containing her lingerie, he placed a typed letter in a sealed envelope. He had to be careful not to say anything incriminating that might be printed in a scandal sheet someday if Rose wanted revenge. But he still needed to let her know how much he wanted her back. So he wrote a cryptic business letter, hoping that she understood what he was really saying.

Dear Ms. Alvarez,

It has been a great pleasure working with you. Your valuable services as a Research Assistant are keenly missed. I have decided not to hire a replacement for this position, as I hope that you (and your cat) will consider returning at some future date under a new and more attractive employment agreement.

This would include an increase in pay, paid educational leave with tuition assistance, a vehicle for your use and a severance package upon completion of your college degree and employment in your chosen field.

I am returning the funds you left to pay for the items you damaged by mistake, as I regret that I also damaged in our last meeting a personal item of yours. Yours was of greater value and irreplaceable. My sincere apologies.

Should you decide not to return to my employment, I will happily provide a positive letter of reference.

With best wishes for your success and happiness, I remain always,

Sincerely Yours,
Eric Weber

****

Rose didn't show the letter to Jack. All she said was that Eric apologized, asked her to come back home and offered to pay for college.

****

The next morning, allowing himself to feel cheerful, Eric cleaned himself up, put on a dress shirt and slacks and waited for Ms. Odom. He loaded Rose's things in her car and shook Ms. Odom's hand. "Thank you for helping Rose. I'm relieved that she's safe and well."

Eric waited at home by the phone every day, hoping Rose would call. Even if she told him to drop dead, it would be some relief to know, one way or the other.

When Rose opened her luggage and read Eric's letter, she wept. "I can go home!" she shouted. "I can go home! And he's going to pay for me to go to college!"

Steven encouraged Rose to stay a week more. "You have the high ground, Honey." he said. "He feels really bad about putting you out and he's offering expensive goodies to get you to come back home. Let him stew for a week longer and he might offer a few little baubles from Tiffany's."

"I would have gone back for nothing at all. He just needed to say 'come home.' I appreciate what you and your sister have done for me, but I really want to go home. Noreen's apartment was perfect, but I don't want to live all alone again." Steven's advice stayed with her, though.

A week later, Rose rang Eric's doorbell and waited on the porch with her cat and suitcases, even though she still had a key. The taxi driver had carried everything up for her, and she gave him a generous tip.

Rose knew it was a big risk coming back. He might hurt her again. Abusive men usually say they're sorry with presents and promises never to hit again. But it was worth the risk for a chance to go to college. And besides, she was lonely and missed him. It was partly her fault anyway. She pushed him too far. The house was big enough that she could stay out of his way when he looked angry. That's how she avoided her father.

Evelyn was gone running errands, so Eric answered the door himself. The sight of Rose made his heart leap. He opened his mouth but couldn't speak.

"What kind of car?" she asked coolly, looking out at the garden.

"What?"

"You said I could have a car for my use. What kind of car?" She still wasn't looking at him.

"I was thinking a used Ford or Chevy compact," he teased, trying not to smile. He missed her bantering and bargaining for everything.

She turned to look at him, raised her eyebrows and blinked at him slowly. "Well, I guess that can be a starting point for negotiations."

****

Rose didn't tell Jack about how she "negotiated" her way into the car of her dreams. As far as she was concerned, it was just a business deal; but Jack would surely see it otherwise.

Eric stepped out of the doorway and she came in with Precious. "Let's discuss it further in the bedroom," she said. It had been over two weeks and she missed his bed. Just seeing him again made her body hot. She put Precious on the floor and headed up the stairs. She made up her mind that she would not argue with him ever again, no matter what, but she felt that she could do some gentle bargaining for the best compensation possible.

"Rose, we can't negotiate an employment agreement in bed."

"Why not?"

"I could end up broke. Rose, wait. Please forgive me. I am so sorry. I swear on my life that I will never hit you ever again, as long as I live."

"A promise like that should come with serious collateral."

"Like what?"

She stopped on the stairs and turned to look at him. "A Mercedes convertible."

"You are a cross between Cruella de Ville and Gordon Gekko," he said impatiently, with his hands on his hips.

"Oh, Mr. Weber, you flatter me," she said, smiling flirtatiously and batting her eyelashes at him down below. She allowed her coat to fall off to the floor, revealing a whisper sheer black lace garter belt and stockings with a matching bra, but no panties. Eric moaned at the sight of her. "A Mercedes convertible?" she repeated slowly with a big smile, then turned and continued up the stairs to his bedroom. She walked up slowly, allowing Eric time to fully appreciate the view.

"Oh, hell," he exhaled in defeat as he climbed the stairs to her. "What color do you want?"

CHAPTER 32

Spring was near, and the days were growing warmer. Rose walked with Eric in the garden while he talked to Otis the gardener and handyman about work that needed to be done outside. Rose's cat trotted close behind, exploring the flower beds and pouncing on bugs.

Otis pointed out plants that didn't survive the winter, areas that needed paint or repairs, trees to be trimmed of dead branches and the mossy brick walkways that had to be pressure washed. Eric approved everything that needed to be done.

"This is a very big house for just one man. Why did you buy it?" she asked Eric.

"What I liked best about it was that it had high ceilings and big doorways. I'm a big guy and I love the feeling of big rooms and space for big furniture. Tall men get used to walking around with their necks bent to avoid ceiling fans and low doorways, but in this house, I don't have to duck. And I like to entertain and throw big parties. I wanted it especially for Mardi Gras. When I lived in a condo, I had four-day parties from Saturday to Fat Tuesday, with friends sleeping on the floor and sofas. I have almost unlimited room here. If it's crowded inside, party guests can sit on the porch or walk in the gardens."

"You haven't had any parties since I've been here. It's getting close to Mardi Gras. Are you going to have a party this year?"

"I don't know. If we have sleepover guests, my young 'godchild' will have to sleep in her own room the whole weekend."

"We'll live," she chuckled. "Let's have a big blow-out bash and have a house full of people." She tucked her hand in the crook of his arm and he smiled in agreement.

Planning for the Mardi Gras party started early the next morning because time was short. Evelyn already knew the routine and starting making her regular to-do list.

Eric personally called to invite his regular overnight friends, then he and Rose addressed and mailed printed invitations for others to attend the afternoon open house parties. He had a different guest list for each day so that he could include as many different people as possible. They were business associates, local friends, young fraternity brothers from Tulane, Saints football players, musicians and a variety of people who were weird enough to be interesting.

A uniformed maid and bartender from a temp agency would be on hand to assist the guests as needed and keep the rooms neat. A full cleaning crew would be sent in when the party was over on Ash Wednesday.

Evelyn had the caterer come to the house to plan the four-day menu, including a morning daily delivery of warming bins of scrambled eggs, grits, biscuits, shrimp or crab crepes, hash browns and bacon for the twelve sleepover guests' breakfasts.

By lunch time, when open house guests would arrive, the caterer would make a second delivery of a variety of hot and cold finger foods, party sandwiches, jambalaya, mini crawfish pies, vegetable trays, cheese trays, assorted dips and spreads, fancy sweets, cakes and pies.

No sit-down suppers would be prepared, because guests would be away at the night parades or partying at some favorite music spot downtown. If any parades were cancelled in case of rain, Evelyn would have gallons of gumbo in the fridge she could heat up in a hurry for supper.

Cases of soft drinks, beer, wine, bottled water, liquor and mixers would be delivered to the back porch, with Otis on hand each morning with tubs of ice to start cooling them down. Eric bought a commercial ice maker and had it installed in the garage for his party, to make sure they would never run short. The liquor store would also provide champagne for the breakfast Mimosas and gallons of Bloody Mary mix for the sleepover guests who preferred something spicier in the morning.

For those who wanted something warm to chase away the chills after the night parades, the bartender would serve Irish coffee, regular coffee, hot cocoa and warm brandy.

Eric's traditional Mardi Gras house party is something like a football tailgate event held inside, minus all rules of civilized behavior. Guests show up with faces painted and wearing costumes. Some wear the familiar Mardi Gras purple, green and gold striped sweatshirts, with long strings of plastic beads of the same colors around their necks. They eat, drink, sing, dance, chant, laugh and raise holy hell. When guests make the rounds meeting and greeting each other, everybody gets a hug or kiss on the cheek. Friends are called by nicknames and friendly insults; newcomers are called by terms of affection such as Honey, Sweetie or Dawlin' because new names are forgotten after a few drinks. Yankees and jealous spouses are taken aback by this much familiarity at first, but most get over it.

The mansion's eight guest rooms were occupied by Rose, five couples and two single men. Eric and Rose greeted each guest as they arrived late on Saturday morning and Eric made introductions. The temp agency maid escorted them to their assigned rooms to leave their luggage. The bartender took care of the drinks until everyone left for the night parades.

Guests arrived by taxi and the two single men, Joel and Larry, (both recently divorced) arrived at the same time by streetcar, because parking on the street during Mardi Gras weekend was totally impossible. Trying to drive through the city was nearly impossible, too. Streets were blocked off all over for smaller neighborhood parades and the open streets were jammed with slow-moving traffic.

Rose recognized one of the single men when they arrived. Joel, a short man with glasses, was a former one-night stand. He recognized her as well. Rose struggled to keep calm as introductions were made. Joel was a hateful s.o.b. who enjoyed making women feel like trash, and it would be like him to announce her secrets to other guests. Her stomach turned to jelly when Joel smiled lecherously at her and said, "Ms. Alvarez, you look familiar. Have we met before?"

"No, I'm sure I would remember you," she said graciously.

“And of course I would remember a beautiful woman like you.”

“Let me show you to your rooms,” Eric said with a broad smile and a pat on the back. He pointed his friend Larry to the room next to Rose and went into the other empty bedroom with Joel. Eric closed the bedroom door and leaned his back against it.

“What’s up, Buddy?” Joel asked with a nervous smile.

“You and Rose know each other,” Eric said.

“You got it all wrong, Eric. I was just trying to be sociable.”

“No. I could see it in both of you right away. And I could see the tension in her body. Whatever went between you in the past, it’s making her uncomfortable.”

“You want me to leave, or what?”

“The kid had a tough time after her parents died. I want her to have fun this weekend and enjoy the party.” Eric folded his arms and looked down at his short friend. “You might be able to help her relax by having as little interaction with her as possible. Avoid looking at her. Don’t get near her. Don’t talk to her unless she talks to you first. Relax and have a good time with the rest of our friends and I think Rose will relax, too. If that doesn’t work, you will get an urgent phone call from home and you will leave immediately. If you breathe a word about knowing Rose to anyone, I will forget that we were ever friends and I will break your bones into very small pieces.”

“Eric, honestly, I just met her at a club one time. Nothing happened between us. Nothing!”

"I'm sure you didn't touch her, Joel, because my godchild is still a minor." He gave Joel a threatening look.

Eric left Joel's room without another word and bounced happily down the stairs as if nothing had happened. The afternoon party ended when it was time for Eric to shoo the crowd of about forty people out the door to go the Endymion Parade.

****

"When your father said he knew my aunt and uncle in Chalmette," Rose told Jack, "I remembered that guy Joel from the Mardi Gras party. I knew sooner or later somebody would recognize me again and you would know all of my secrets and hate me for deceiving you. On top of that, some people from my past turned out to be dangerous."

CHAPTER 33

Standing out on the street for hours that late at night, everyone was cold, hungry and tired. Evelyn had a fire going in every fireplace, the beds turned down in every room and hot cocoa waiting in the kitchen. Some of the friends were drunk and had to be poured into bed, but most stayed up late eating, drinking, shooting pool and catching up on each other's lives since they were together last. Joel and Larry were the only guests who stayed downtown after the parade so they could look for girls.

Later, Eric asked Rose if she had a good time today partying with his friends.

"A *great* time! I love your friends. I never knew people like them. They're good and nice and happy. They're smart and have good jobs and families. Do you think they could tell that I never went to high school?"

"The frat boys your age didn't seem to notice."

"Humph. Frat boys don't notice anything but tits and ass. What about the grownups?"

"Oh, they though your tits and ass were wonderful, too. And they thought you were very smart. A charming young lady."

Most of the guests slept late on Sunday morning. Rose and Eric came downstairs early to be good hosts to the other early birds. After a buffet breakfast, all scattered to go shopping, sightseeing or partying in the Quarter.

Eric and Rose stayed home to relax until it was time to host the afternoon open house. Rose did some research on the invited guests and learned something about nearly all of them. Eric was impressed that she chatted easily with everyone as though she knew them well and served as a charming hostess. She paid extra attention to guests who were neither rich nor famous, to make sure they felt as though they were.

The over-nighters who went downtown earlier in the day agreed that they would meet to watch the Bacchus Parade together at a designated spot on Canal Street. Days were mild but evenings turned chilly, so Eric brought along a big thermos of coffee to keep them all warm. Rose brought a department store shopping bag full of leftover sandwiches and snacks from the buffet. Only newcomers thought they could get something to eat on a parade route.

Little by little, the friends came from different directions, snaking their way through the crowds to get to Eric and Rose. It took a couple of hours for the huge parade to travel along its parade route from Napoleon Avenue to Canal Street, so parade watchers near the end of the route passed the time by having a street party.

While they were waiting, Rose was spotted by several homeless girlfriends. She signaled them a quick "no," usually meaning that she was in a good set-up with a guy and didn't want to be recognized.

They understood and moved on.

As the parade neared, the crowds pushed in tight, packed shoulder to shoulder from the curb to the storefront behind them. The noise from the marching bands and the screaming thousands of people reverberated off the walls. It was impossible to talk or hear anything.

Sonny and two of his friends came up behind Rose and eased her to the back of the crowd so they could talk. Eric was having fun and didn't notice until she was gone, then pushed through the crowd until he got to her again. He glared at the boys and put his arm protectively around Rose.

"It's okay, Eric. Sonny is a friend from the homeless shelter," she shouted to be heard over the noise. "Sonny, this is my godfather Mr. Eric Weber."

"I'm sorry to bother you, but I recognized Rose and saw she had food she was handing out. Me and Slack and Peso haven't eat all day. Could we have a sandwich?"

"Of course you can," Rose said, and gave them each one from her shopping bag. She discretely motioned them to go away, which they did.

The three boys spread out in the dense crowd to earn their living. Sonny sold small single hits of cocaine. Slack bummed cigarettes from smokers to distract them while Peso picked their pockets. Peso got the wallet of an undercover cop, and with lightning speed handed it off to Slack. The cop grabbed Peso while his partner went after Slack. Slack kept his stash in his coat, so he pulled it off and dumped it into Rose's shopping bag before the cop got close enough to see what happened.

Slack and Peso were both handcuffed while loudly protesting "I ain't done nothin'!" Parade watchers forgot about the floats and turned to watch the arrests behind them.

Peso said to the cop, "Our friends Rose and Eric right there, they'll tell you. They know us. We ain't thieves. You got it wrong!"

Peso's captor, Detective Rouse, asked Eric and Rose if they knew either of the boys. Rose answered, "They came around earlier asking for some sandwiches, that's all."

The officer holding onto Slack spotted the discarded coat in Rose's shopping bag. "Is that your bag?"

"Yes," she answered.

"That's the coat this kid was wearing. He handed it off to this lady and she hid it for him. You'll have to come with us, Ma'am," he said to Rose.

"Can we just get away from this crowd and talk about this, Officer?" Eric asked politely. "We can straighten this out, I'm sure."

The officer directed them off Canal Street to a side street where there were no people and less noise. All of Eric's friends went with them to see what was going on. Both of the cops looked worried about being surrounded. "Step back, folks!" one ordered.

"These are our houseguests for the weekend. There will be no trouble, I assure you," Eric said politely. "This is my godchild, Rose Alvarez."

Eric asked Rose, "Did the kid hand you his coat?"

"No, I didn't know it was in the shopping bag until the officer saw it."

"Did you touch it at any time?" Eric asked.

"No, never."

"Officer," Eric said, "if the kid handed it to her and she hid it in the bag for him, her fingerprints would be on the vinyl, wouldn't they?"

The officer nodded.

"You have the coat. Rose and I will go down to the station in the morning and she will give you her fingerprints. She couldn't have stashed the coat without touching it, right?"

"Are you a lawyer?" the cop asked.

Eric laughed. "No, Sir. I'm Eric Weber. I'm a writer. I own the old Keen Mansion on St. Charles Avenue." Eric showed them his driver's license.

"How do you uptown folks know these punks anyway?"

"Rose has a soft heart for these homeless teenagers. She's always giving them food or a few dollars. They all know her by name."

"Okay," the cop said. "You all look like respectable citizens. Ms. Alvarez, you come down and give us your fingerprints tomorrow." He gave her his card. "Ask for me."

The two plain clothes officers took the two boys to a waiting patrol car and drove away.

Eric, Rose and their friends all wanted to leave the parade after that. "There's enough of us here, we'll be our own parade walking down The Avenue, huh, Rose?" Larry asked. "We even have beads to throw!"

Some of the friends started singing *Big Chief* and *Iko Iko* as they strutted parade style down the street toward home, sipping their beers or Hurricanes as they danced around.

One of the wives walking close to Eric and Rose said, "You try to help these street kids, Rose, but you can't really. They're hopeless."

"I don't agree," Eric said. "Rose and I believe that people can change if someone shows them kindness. We've both seen it happen, haven't we?"

"Yeah, a couple of really hard cases got turned around. They're happy and doing great now," she said smiling up at Eric.

Sonny followed the group a far distance back so he wouldn't be noticed. He wanted to know where Rose was living in case he ever needed money or a place to hide out.

CHAPTER 34

The day before Mardi Gras is Lundi Gras, or Fat Monday. The day begins early with the downtown arrival by boat of the black King of Carnival, King Zulu and his royal court. It becomes a street party like no other on earth, with music, food and dancing in the streets.

All of the guests were up and ready to go to Canal Street by seven o'clock, eager to see the parades and the outrageous costumes people were wearing in the Quarter. A slight chance of rain was expected late in the afternoon, so Eric handed out little pocket-sized ponchos to the guests as they went out the door.

Eric took Rose to the police station to give her fingerprints, then went home to welcome the day's open house guests.

A light misty drizzle didn't deter anybody downtown from continuing with the drinking and dancing in the street, but it turned into a hard blowing rain by five o'clock. Thousands of tourists ran for shelter under every awning and into every restaurant, bar and souvenir shop in the area. The Weber party finally gave up trying to get inside anywhere, and all headed back to Eric's house to change out of their wet clothes and warm up. Along the way, they picked up several more people they knew and invited them back to Eric's house. Wet shoes, socks and ponchos were shed in the foyer and guests were handed fresh towels before coming inside.

The catered buffet was overflowing with jambalaya, hot French bread, Irish coffee, and a dozen or so trays of finger foods, meats, cheeses, fancy pastries, hot and cold dips and King Cake. Eric put on Mardi Gras, Cajun and Zydeco music for dancing, and to keep the party spirit going. He had made a special CD of both old and new rain songs just in case, and the old Irma Thomas song *It's Rainin'* was the favorite. Everyone in the house knew the words and sang along. Some of them went out to the porch to dance and sing it loud to the neighbors, daring the storm to dampen the party mood.

Party guests danced, shot pool, snuggled by the fire, talked, told jokes, sang and ate and drank until late at night.

The weather on Fat Tuesday was pleasant enough. Not too cold, with clear sunny skies. Everyone was out of the house and headed to the all-day parades downtown by ten o'clock in the morning. Eric and Rose came back home at two in the afternoon to host the open house party. Friends came in and out all afternoon and night. Most were invited, but others just showed up and were welcome. Most of the over-nighters didn't straggle back in until midnight, the official end of the carnival season and the beginning of Lent.

All of the guests started their trips back to their own homes before noon on Ash Wednesday. As they left, Eric called each one of the guys by his old nickname from their college days. They were Skeeter, Mutt, Zap, 'Bama, Snake, Slick and Nunzey. Rose didn't tell Jack what Eric's nickname was. They all called Eric "Shorty," and Jack would want to know why.

"How does a guy who's six feet six get the nickname Shorty?" Rose asked Eric when they were finally back in bed together that night.

"It started with a girl I was dating in college. She called me Shorty because of this joke that was going around back then about a tall guy who was nicknamed Shorty."

"Tell me the joke."

"Well, there was a tall guy that everybody called Shorty because a former girlfriend had written on his penis the word 'Shorty' with a permanent marker. He had many, many female admirers, so obviously the word 'Shorty' didn't imply that he was poorly equipped. None of Shorty's girlfriends would tell. One of the guys persuaded a girl to sleep with Shorty and then come back and tell him the secret. After sleeping with Shorty, she came back to give her report. She said that the full inscription on Shorty's penis was Shorty's Bar and Grill, Chattanooga, Tennessee."

Rose laughed so hard her ribs hurt. "That certainly applies to you, Shorty!"

CHAPTER 35

Rose completed her GED classes and got her high school diploma that spring. She was reluctantly accepted to Tulane University, Eric's old alma mater, for the fall semester, but only because Eric pulled out all the stops to get her in. The university's high standards for acceptance definitely did *not* include GED students, ever, only regular high school graduates with exceptional records of achievement, evidence of leadership abilities, community service and special skills or talents. But Rose's "special skills" couldn't be listed on a résumé.

Eric's grandfather graduated from the medical school and was a life-long benefactor to Tulane. Weber Hall was named for Eric's father, the principal donor for the construction. Eric had also been generous with his time and money, contributing large amounts to the athletic program every year. When he went to football games, he was invited to sit on the bench with the team. A lot of older fans still remembered him as a star player, the biggest lineman they ever had. Eric called in favors from everywhere. Pressure was put on the school from many influential sources to get them to accept

Rose, which they did. The official letter of acceptance stated that she was admitted because of her exceptionally high SAT scores and her "disadvantaged early childhood."

"Do you want me to stay in the dorm?" she asked Eric cautiously. She remembered that Eric told his travel planner Margaret Rose would stay with him until she started college. "You could get back to writing again and travel wherever you need to go while I'm at school." She wanted him to know she would leave the decision up to him, if that was what he still wanted. But Eric and Evelyn were like family and she didn't really want to leave them.

That silent voice that only he could hear spoke in a whisper to him again. "Let her go," the voice said. Eric shook his head and said a loud NO to the voice.

"Good," Rose answered, thinking he was speaking to her. "But you do want to get back to the adventures of Cade Monroe, don't you?"

"The man at the bar in Cozumel told me to let her go. The voice said to let her go."

"I can't let her go," he mumbled to himself.

"Are you talking to yourself?"

"Um, yeah. I was thinking out loud about the next book. I have it sort of outlined in my head, but we'll have to go the Andes Mountains for about a month for me to do some research before I get started on it."

"Mountains! I've never been to any mountains. That'll be fun."

"Fun? We won't be in a fancy mountain lodge, Rose. We'll be hiking to remote places and sleeping in tents."

"I'm up for an adventure if you are."

Eric's publisher was calling him regularly and pressuring him to get started on his next novel. The series of books with the Cade Monroe character as the action hero was enormously popular, and readers were clamoring for more. Eric's agent got the publisher to offer a much bigger advance this time, so Eric agreed.

"Rosie," Eric said, "when it's fall here in New Orleans, it's spring in the Andes Mountains. I'd like you to come with me, but you'd have to delay starting school until the following semester."

"A trip to South America is an education in itself. I wouldn't miss it. Whoo-hoo!" she said, hugging Eric around the ribs. Rose did her happy dance around the room, chanting *Second Line*, and making Eric grin. Her joy was infectious.

"I might be able to get our guide and interpreter to rent some horses and take us to remote villages," he said. "Have you ever ridden a horse?"

Rose said that the only time she was ever close to a horse was when she saw them in Mardi Gras parades, but she willing to give it a try. Eric made arrangements for Rose to get riding lessons at Cypress Bend Horse Farm and Riding Academy out in the country on River Road. It was owned and operated by Jerry Denson and Brenda Allemand, who had excellent reputations in their community.

On their first day of lessons, Savannah LeBlanc Melancon was there, exercising her horse Stormy. Savannah was one of the richest women in the state and owner of LeBlanc Plantation. Eric had known Savannah and her husband Wayne for at least ten years, having many friends in common and socializing with them at various parties and fund-raising events.

Eric and Savannah greeted each other as old friends. "So, you're back in town again!" she said with a laugh. "It's hard to keep sending you invitations when you're gone so much. How long will you be here? I'll throw us a party at the house before you can leave the country again."

"Actually, I'm giving a big party myself before I leave again, for that young lady over there with Brenda. I'll send *you* an invitation."

Savannah looked at Rose and gave Eric a critical look. "Really, Eric? A bit young, even for you."

"Rose is my godchild, Savannah. Her parents died recently and she didn't have any blood relatives who would take her in. With nowhere to go, she showed up at my house and I took her in. What else could I do? She's living with me until she starts college and then I'll be on the road again. So, how's your family?"

"Both Amy and Albert are happily married. No grandchildren yet. Wayne's production of New Orleans Riversong is going over very well at the Saenger. He's thrilled, of course. I'll have Wayne send you and Rose tickets."

"By the way, Brenda and Jerry, the owners here, are our closest friends. Brenda is a life-long rider and you can be sure that Rose will be okay with her." Rose continued riding lessons all summer, driving herself there in her new convertible, while Eric kept busy with friends and his former activities.

Before they left for Chile, Rose and Eric went to see his friend's musical production at the Saenger Theater and walked the two blocks down Canal Street to the Ritz Carlton for a late supper with Savannah and Wayne.

Eric threw a first-class cocktail party for all the people who helped get Rose accepted at Tulane University, so that Rose could thank each one personally. He invited friends, celebrities and athletes as well, to add to the excitement of the evening. Every person was enchanted with Rose, who was on her best behavior. She chatted easily with the brightest and the best, as well as the stuffiest and most boring of the academics.

Eric provided the very best of everything to introduce Rose into the college community, including a popular young musical quartet for dancing. The evening was a smashing success. Everyone wished Rose success at college and Eric success with his forthcoming book.

CHAPTER 36

Eric's preliminary research of Chile offered some promising scenarios for his book. San Pedro de Atacama, a small town on the edge of the Atacama Desert, would be their base of operations. From there, they could reach both the high mountains and the Pacific Coast.

Rose was the trip photographer, documenting the flora and fauna, geology, people and culture of the area. While Eric wrote down story ideas in the evening, Rose sat with their guide and interpreter to learn as much as she could. She understood a little Spanish from her street friends in New Orleans, but being immersed in it helped her to pick it up quickly. She was a natural.

Eric had virtually zero ability to speak or understand any foreign language. He never could develop an ear for it. "Next time we go to a foreign country," he told Rose, "I'm going to get you a foreign language course ahead of time and *you* can be our interpreter."

"Proud to be of service on the expedition, Captain," she said with a snappy salute.

They visited abandoned copper mines and the towns where the workers once lived. They were allowed to visit some active mining operations, because the companies that owned them gave special permission. A famous writer like Eric Weber was no ordinary tourist, and the managers on site were happy to help him out, show him how their massive equipment worked and answer all of his questions. One lucky fellow was assigned to accompany the beautiful Ms. Alvarez and assure her comfort and safety while she took photographs.

"These locations will be great places for Cade Monroe to chase bad guys and get into all kinds of danger," Eric commented to her. "Maybe the bad guys will try to squash him like a bug with one of the gigantic earth movers."

"But a beautiful girl will save him just in time," Rose suggested.

"They always do," he said ruefully, smiling at her.

The thin air of the high elevation made it difficult for Eric and Rose to get enough oxygen, so they tired easily. They rested often during the day and slept longer at night. They had to return to lower elevations to recuperate from time to time, so they took the opportunity to visit the Pan de Azúcar (sugar loaf) National Park on the Pacific Coast.

Their guide and driver helped them unload all of their food, water and supplies, then left. Eric and Rose camped in a tent on the wide beach, away from the water and the other campsites. They were relatively alone and had both the privacy and oxygen for sexual recreation. They stayed on the beach for three glorious days of sunshine and splashing in shallow water along the shore. The altitude, lack of clouds and total darkness made for the best romantic stargazing at night.

From the national park, their driver took them to the southern Atacama to see the rare event of the flowering of the desert.

"The Atacama is the highest and driest desert on earth, with about half an inch of rain a year, at most," the local guide told them. "El Niño brought us a little rain and ended an eight year drought. You are so lucky to be here at this time! People will come from all over the world to see this." It was a spectacular sea of red, blue, purple, white and yellow flowers extending for miles! "There are two hundred kinds of flowers here in the Atacama, and some can't grow anywhere else on earth. So the government of Chile protects them from being damaged or picked by visitors. You *must* stay on the walking path, or the security guards will arrest you," he warned.

Eric thought his novel would have to include some lunatic or terrorist trying to destroy the flowers and blaming it on some sweet innocent very sexy female botanist.

Eric and Rose could hardly believe their good luck and perfect timing to be in the desert to see this rare event. It was breathtaking.

"You promised to show me the most beautiful places on earth," Rose said to Eric. "This has to be one of them."

"And we're just getting started!" he said. "I will show you the whole world!"

They went back to their home base at the town and waited for their reservations at the Paranal Observatory. "We have weekend reservations, meals included," Rose read from the observatory's literature. "Base camp is at 8,000 feet and we have to walk up 500 feet more to get to the telescope. I think Cade Monroe could have some hot romance at the overnight center and some thrilling cliffhangers at 8,000 feet," she said to Eric.

"Will you give me some ideas or inspiration while we're up there for the hot sex scenes in the book?"

"Ideas and demonstrations! I can hardly wait to see what the stars look like from up there."

Photographs were allowed throughout the telescope's facility, so Rose got a hundred or so great shots of the visitor center, computer control room, the giant telescope itself and views of the surrounding mountains.

After stargazing on the mountain top, they spent a few more days hiking and horseback riding around the area of San Pedro, until the shuttle bus service took them to the nearest airport at Calama. From there, they flew to Santiago for a week of sightseeing, a winery tour, nightclubbing and shopping. Rose especially loved the famous Chilean Folklore dinner show, with great local cuisine and the colorful stage performance.

CHAPTER 37

Rose started her freshman year of college in the spring semester, majoring in business and finance, and started swimming lessons at the university pool. As promised, Eric gave her a generous increase in pay and paid for all of her tuition, fees and books. While she was at school during the day, he started writing his next book, *Atacama*.

Rose was disappointed that she had a great wardrobe for college, but even the richest students dressed like the homeless kids in the French Quarter. So she dressed in cutoffs and tee shirts like everyone else to fit in. But she still stood out from the crowd when she hopped into her $85,000 silver blue Mercedes SL Roadster convertible to drive home.

While Eric was working, Rose went with a few college girlfriends to hang out and shop at Lakeside Mall. A girl in her early teens ambled by and immediately caught Rose's attention, because the girl was wearing Rose's blouse. She recognized her little rose pin Eric bought her that was still on it.

Rose gasped. "That girl broke into our house and stole my blouse! While we were gone? Is anything else missing?"

Rose caught up with the girl. "Excuse me, but I just love that blouse you're wearing. Where did you buy it? I'd like to get one. Do they come in different colors?"

"I didn't buy it. It was a present from my boyfriend Sonny and I don't know where he bought it. Sorry."

"That's okay," Rose said sweetly. "What's your name?"

"Misty," she said.

"Thanks anyway, Misty. Have a nice day!"

"So Sonny broke into our house and stole my blouse for his girlfriend. He's a pro. I didn't even notice it was missing. I wonder how often he's been there. Better not tell Eric about it. He'll go crazy and want to kill Sonny."

Taking from strangers as a way of surviving on the street was understandable. But you don't take from friends. Rose realized sadly that Sonny was no longer a friend.

Rose hunted down Sonny in the Quarter one afternoon, offered to buy him lunch and casually mentioned that she and Eric would be taking a little weekend trip to do a book signing in Atlanta.

The day that they were leaving town, she made an anonymous call to the NOPD.

"My neighbors and I on this block have noticed things missing when we've been away. Not a big burglary that you would report. Just little things that you might not miss right away. A strange-looking kid was seen watching houses in this area today and we're leaving town. I'm afraid he might be the one. Could you have someone watch the neighborhood and look out for him after dark?"

Rose baited the rat trap, set it and alerted the cat. Cops in an unmarked car waited out of sight that night. Sonny the rat took the bait, and the cops took Sonny.

Evelyn was awakened from a sound sleep at two in the morning by police officers banging on the front door and ringing the bell. She was shocked to see two officers holding a bizarre-looking young man in handcuffs.

The police told Evelyn that Sonny was caught breaking in and she should notify her employer what happened. Nothing in the house was damaged, but the owner should take precautions to make sure that nobody else could get in the same way. Evelyn phoned Eric in Atlanta immediately. She reassured the boss that she was a bit shook up, but otherwise fine.

Sonny served a short term in the Youth Study Center, a euphemistic name for the Orleans Parish lockup for teens. He was convicted for breaking and entering and theft. The bleeding heart Juvenile Court judge thought he could be rehabilitated and was lenient on him. Sonny learned a lot from his pals in juvie and came out a much more ambitious criminal than when he went in.

CHAPTER 38

When he got out, Sonny hooked up with Dago, his former cocaine customer. Dago was a scary looking guy. His close-set eyes were lifeless and had dark shadows all around them. He had no eyebrows. He looked angry and impatient all the time, ready to strike. Dago had served time in Parish Prison and learned some handy things while he was there. He told Sonny he didn't need to deal drugs anymore. Dago had a sure fire plan for robbing convenience stores, and he needed a partner.

A former utility lineman in Parish Prison told him how easy it was to disable a power transformer quickly and quietly. A few sparks and little flashes of light, and the whole neighborhood went dark, including street lights, cameras and alarms. The lineman tried it and went in to rob a store with a flashlight, but the light was seen from outside and he got caught.

Dago had a better plan than the lineman. He'd knock out the transformer like the guy taught him, but he would use night vision goggles to rob the place. He scored a couple pairs of the goggles cheap from a man who needed cash in a hurry. Dago and Sonny would be able to see everything with the goggles, but nobody in the store or outside could see them to put up a fight or to identify them later. Dago also bought two stolen pistols from a friend in the gun trade. Dago said they would have to wear all black clothes and go on a night when there was no moon, so it would be totally dark outside. Dago was smart. He thought of everything.

They selected their first target, an all-night liquor store in a quiet part of town. It was nine o'clock on a Sunday night, when there was nobody in the store except the store owner and his wife.

Sonny waited near the store while Dago blew out the transformer a block away. Sonny put on his goggles and went in as soon as the neighborhood went black. He ordered the store owners to lay face down on the floor, then he waited for Dago to join him.

"We have night vision goggles, so we can see in the dark. If you try anything, man, I'll shoot your wife," Sonny warned them.

Dago was more threatening. He poked the couple in the ribs with his gun. "Feel that, Asshole? If you move a finger, I'll shoot you both in the head! Understand?"

The man and his wife both said yes. "No trouble, no trouble. Take what you want, Mister," the terrified man said. "Don't shoot, please."

Dago emptied the cash register and grabbed a carton of cigarettes.

An armed private security guard from a local warehouse was also in the store that night, getting his usual six-pack from the beer cooler on his way home from work. Sonny and Dago didn't see him on the other side of the tall store displays. He snaked along the floor in the direction of the voices, and when he was close enough to guess where the robbers were, he turned on his flashlight. Sonny and Dago were temporarily blinded by the light hitting their goggles, and cried out in surprise and pain. Their natural response was to turn away from the light. The security guard quickly fired several shots at them. Sonny returned fire blindly and hit the security guard by dumb luck.

Dago was wounded in his right side and dropped the cash and cigarettes. Sonny and Dago both got away before the wounded guard could fire in their direction again. They ran to Dago's car waiting around the corner in the dark. "FUCK!" Dago cried in pain. "I didn't get nothin' but a bullet in the gut, Man! We gotta get outta here. Drive!"

"I know a place where we can hide out, get you patched up *and* get some travelling money to get outta town," Sonny said. "Rose Alvarez, the same ungrateful bitch who sent me to jail. She owes me."

Sonny drove them to St. Charles Avenue and parked away from the house. They were both armed, so they didn't need to sneak in. They went to the front door and rang the bell.

****

"Once again," she told Jack, "my past came back to haunt me. I should have known better than to get close to someone like you and expect to keep my secrets hidden, but I was in complete denial. Now I realize that I need to stick to my own kind."

215

CHAPTER 39

Rose was up late studying. Precious was lying on the table next to her stack of books. Eric was in his office listening to a favorite album with his headphones on and waiting up for Rose to go to bed with him. But he fell asleep before it finished playing. Evelyn had already gone to bed. The doorbell rang and Rose went to get it.

Sonny and Dago were standing there with guns pointed at her. Rose backed up slowly and the two men came in and closed the door quietly. Sonny's friend was bleeding from his side and looking ready to kill anybody who crossed him.

"What are you doing, Sonny?" she asked cautiously. "What do you want? Do you need money?"

"Yeah, we need money. But first you gonna fix up my friend Dago. Where's the old man?"

"Upstairs asleep," she lied. "Old people go to bed early. They aren't night people like us, Sonny. You know that," she said with a smile.

"You give us any problems and he wakes up, I'll shoot him. Understand? So be quiet."

"Sure, Sonny. I'll help you any way I can. Your friend should lie down on the sofa in the front parlor first and then we can go get what I need to patch him up. The first aid things are in the kitchen. Okay?"

She led them to the front parlor, away from Eric's office, and helped Dago lay down with a throw pillow under his head. Dago wasn't a very big man, but he looked dangerous anyway. His dark stringy hair was a filthy mess. His knuckles were scarred and he had tattoos everywhere that Rose could see. When Rose looked directly into his eyes, it gave her a chill in her bones. There was no sign of a conscience or simple humanity in them. It was like looking into a dark and lifeless pit. Precious hopped up on the back of the sofa to get a better look at the stranger. Dago gave her an evil look and she hissed at him.

Sonny went with Rose to the big storage pantry near the kitchen where first aid supplies were kept. She retrieved bandages, antibiotic spray and a bottle of sterile saline. Sonny pushed her impatiently back to the parlor to take care of Dago.

Rose pushed up Dago's bloody tee shirt and wiped away the blood with a gauze pad soaked with saline. "You're lucky. It's a shallow flesh wound. It's bleeding a lot probably because the bullet hit a small blood vessel. The bullet went through. We might be able to slow the bleeding by keeping pressure on the wound. But you need to go to an emergency room for stitches to close it up. You'll keep on losing blood if you don't and you'll eventually pass out," she lied.

"No hospital!" Dago said. "They always call the cops for a bullet wound."

"I know. But I could go with you and say that you were showing me how to clean my gun and I accidently shot you because I didn't know it was loaded." Rose wanted to get them out of the house to protect Eric and Evelyn. She would go with them as a hostage, if necessary.

"Maybe we should wait 'til morning and go to one of them street clinics," Sonny said. "They don't have cops hanging around like at the hospital."

"Your friend could lose a whole lotta blood by morning," Rose lied again. Keeping pressure on it could keep blood loss to a bare minimum until morning, but Rose wanted them scared enough to get moving right away. The longer they hung around, the greater the danger to everybody in the house, especially if Eric heard what was going on and came out of his office. Even worse if he came out with that pistol he keeps in his desk. Rose didn't want anyone to get shot, including Sonny and Dago.

"Get a needle and thread and you stitch him up," Sonny said.

"What? No man! I'm hurtin' bad," Dago complained. "I need something to numb it before getting' sewed up."

"I could do it, Sonny," Rose agreed reluctantly. "It would hurt worse than getting shot and he would probably get a bad infection and die anyway. He needs a doctor and antibiotics." Rose dramatized the situation to scare Dago as much as possible.

Sonny thought about it. "You got a cell phone, Rose?"

"Yeah." She took it from her pocket and handed it to Sonny. He gave it to Dago.

"Dago, you call me on my phone and let me know everything's okay when you get to the hospital. I'm gonna stay here 'til you get back all safe and sound and stitched up. If the cops come here 'cause they don't believe your story, Rosie, the first thing I'm gonna do is shoot your old man and take a few cops with him."

"Don't worry, Sonny. I'll make sure they believe me. I'm a very good liar. I'll drive him to the hospital and pay the bill. He's very weak. Help him out to my car. It's out back." Convinced by Rose that he was mortally wounded, Dago moaned and staggered when he got up. He leaned on Sonny like he was ready to pass out. Rose led the way out of the back door and secretly flipped the automatic lock so the door would lock Sonny outside after she and Dago drove away.

It wasn't necessary though. When the men followed her through the dark kitchen to the back door, Evelyn stepped out of the shadows and shot both men in the back at close range with her little Beretta.

The cat was always at Rose's side, following her through the house wherever she went. The gunshots terrified her. Precious jumped into the air screeching, and ran with fur flying for a place to hide.

Rose fell on the ground in the back yard next to the men, screaming hysterically. Who fired the gun? What was happening? She had a flash back to the day her parents killed each other and she sat in their blood on the floor. All of the terrors of her life came back to her. Rose was in shock. Sonny and Dago dropped their guns in the yard when they fell down and couldn't find them in the dark. Otherwise they would have shot both Rose and Evelyn, who was still standing in the open doorway trembling with fear.

Eric's headphones were silent and the muffled sound of gunfire woke him up. He grabbed his unloaded pistol from his desk and came running. He turned on the kitchen light and spotted Evelyn first. He took the gun from her, put it on the kitchen counter and sat her in a chair before going outside to tend to Rose. She was crying hysterically, so he knew she was alive. The two men were moaning and cursing, so he knew they were alive, too. With the light shining out of the kitchen door, Eric found the other weapons close by and tossed them across the yard in the dark where the two men couldn't get to them. He held Rose close to his chest while he called 911 on his cell phone.

Whispering soothing words of comfort to her, he carried her into the house from the back yard after he finished the call, and laid her on a sofa in the great room. She was glassy-eyed and trembling. He poured a shot of whiskey for her to help her relax and held it while she sipped. She was shaking too much to hold it herself.

"Stay here," he said to Rose. "I'm going back to hold a gun on those guys until the police arrive."

Evelyn was surprisingly calm. While they were waiting, she told Eric the basics of what happened.

When the police arrived, Evelyn and Eric each gave a statement to the police detectives. Eric said he had fallen asleep listening to music in his office with headphones on and didn't know about Sonny and Dago until he heard the muffled sound of gunshots.

"After we had that break-in a while back, my son-in-law was worried about me being alone in this big house so often," Evelyn told them. "So he bought me this little gun and showed me how to use it. I was still awake in my room and I heard Rose talking to one of those men when she went to the pantry for bandages." She walked the detectives through her story, showing them where each thing happened. "I was scared out of my mind, but I knew I had to do something." She was shaking as she spoke, so Eric put his arm around her and held her hand. "I waited in the dark, right over there, and they passed right by me. Very close. I saw that I had a chance to stop both of them at once and not let them kill me or Miss Rose or Mr. Weber, so I did it. I shot them both."

"You did a very brave thing, Evelyn," Eric said, trying to comfort her. Eric told the detectives that he would bring his godchild Rose to the station to give them her statement the following day, as she was in no condition to talk.

A police photographer recorded the crime scene, two ambulances took the wounded away and the detectives bagged and tagged the two guns from the back yard and Evelyn's little Beretta as evidence.

Sonny and Dago both recovered because they were hit with small caliber bullets in non-lethal spots. They were sentenced to twenty years in prison for armed robbery, attempted murder at the liquor store, possession of a firearm by a felon, destruction of public property, criminal trespass, attempted kidnapping of Rose and other charges. They were both sent to the state pen at Angola, generally considered to be one of the lower levels of hell.

Eric was so grateful to Evelyn that he treated her to a first class vacation in Hawaii, and hired a maid service to do the housework so all Evelyn had to do was cook from then on. When she came back from Hawaii, Eric bought her a new car.

Rose later told Eric the whole story about the day her parents died. She had recurring nightmares about her parents and the two thugs, and sometimes woke up in terror. Eric had nightmares, too, now and then, but he didn't tell her about his. They just held each other when they got scared about the past … or the future.

****

"Eric offered some 'incentives' to the police officers to keep his name out of the news," she told Jack. "The newspaper report didn't mention his name, only that two robbery suspects were located in an uptown neighborhood and were treated for injuries sustained during the liquor store robbery. By the time the men went to trial, it was old news and Eric was out of the country."

CHAPTER 40

She climbed up on his lap and snuggled against his chest. He hugged her close and kissed her forehead. "So, Mr. Weber, where do we go for our next Cade Monroe adventure?"

"Nowhere, for a while. We'll relax and do a publicity and book signing tour for *Atacama* before I start something new. Maybe this summer we can escape the New Orleans heat and go someplace north for a while."

"How about London?" she asked excitedly.

"I was thinking of Shreveport," he teased.

Later that night while Eric was taking a shower, he playfully recited an old nursery rhyme to himself with a big grin. "Pussy cat, pussy cat, where have you been? I've been to London to visit the queen." He was almost as excited as Rose about the trip. Despite his many travels, he had never been to London. He and Rose would discover it together.

They returned from a two-week tour of England and Scotland in July and prepared for Rose to begin her sophomore year at Tulane in the Freeman School of Business.

Eric was away from home a lot for various appointments that summer. Rose thought he seemed distracted and disturbed about something, but didn't ask. *"I'll do my best not to aggravate or argue with him and let him deal with whatever it is. I'll just do whatever I can to keep him happy."*

Eric went to see his doctor, his attorney, his accountant and his bank. Instead of taking time for relaxing and doing a publicity tour, Eric put Rose in the hands of Jack Monroe and left for Israel.

CHAPTER 41

Rose finished telling her story to Jack, omitting sensitive details from time to time to be loyal to Eric's memory and to avoid hurting Jack unnecessarily. He had remained silent throughout, as promised.

"At the time, I didn't feel at all guilty about our arrangement. I enjoyed it. I felt safe here. Eric was nice to me and we were two of a kind. It was like a business partnership. He got what he needed and I got what I needed. It was only after Eric left the country and I fell in love with you that I felt ashamed of the life I had been living."

"I tried to keep up the charade until the day I met your family. Kyle and your dad knew my Uncle Joe and Aunt Claudette. I knew immediately that, sooner or later, you would meet somebody like Eric's friend Joel who would recognize me and tell you that I was a liar, thief, con artist and common alley cat." Rose sat quietly for a while, relieved that she got all the way through it.

"I'm done now. You can say something if you want to," she told Jack.

After a long silence, Jack said, "Eric was legendary for his sexual prowess. You didn't learn it from books, did you? He was the one who taught you about making love.”

“No,” Rose said. “Eric taught me about sex. *You* taught me about making love. And I didn’t fall in love with Eric. I fell in love with you.”

He got up from the sofa and went to take Rose into his arms. He kissed her on the forehead. “I don’t hate you. I’m not ashamed of you. I still love you and want to marry you. If you’ll let me, I’d like to come back tomorrow and share with you all of *my* family secrets. Then we’ll both know the whole truth about each other. I don’t want to start on that tonight. Let’s get some rest and I’ll come back tomorrow. Okay?”

Rose nodded and tears filled her eyes.

CHAPTER 42

Jack returned on Saturday morning at 10:00. He and Rose went to the front parlor to continue talking.

"I'll start at the beginning, as you did. My grandfather, William Monroe, worked as the bookkeeper at a small local fish dock that sold seafood to the public and local restaurants. Back then, it was almost a total cash business, easy for the manager to skim a little for himself now and then. Grandfather was more ambitious than that. Over the years he worked there, he embezzled $47,000. The nice house he and Grandma owned was purchased for not even a fourth of that, so his take was a *lot* of money back then. One day, he disappeared with his loot, abandoning his wife Shirley and son John (my father) without a word. Grandma Shirley lost the family home, moved into a cheap apartment and went to work cleaning houses to support herself and Dad. Dad dropped out of school as soon as he was old enough to get work."

"Shirley was an attractive woman and one of her bachelor customers tried to seduce her. She refused and he beat her up so badly she couldn't

227

work for a long time and her other customers dropped her. The man who beat her up was found at home with his throat cut the next day. The police suspected that my father killed him, but there wasn't enough evidence to prove it. Dad's knife was at the bottom of the Mississippi River, there were no witnesses and DNA evidence wasn't heard of back then. The case was never solved, but Grandma Shirley told me that Dad told her he did it."

"In the meantime, Grandpa William became a bigamist and married a woman in Natchez without divorcing Shirley. His second wife knew all along he was wanted by the police for theft, but she loved him anyway. However, when she found out that he had a wife in New Orleans and a black mistress across town, she turned him in. Grandpa died of influenza in prison."

"Dad eventually got a good steady job working for a building contractor. He learned all of the trades. Carpentry, painting, plastering, landscaping. Grandma kept house and Dad took care of them both."

"My mother, Wanda Kincade, was married before she met my dad. She was drop dead gorgeous as a young woman and worked as a stripper at a club on Bourbon Street. She really drew in the crowds! Patrons at the bar gave her generous tips, too. The club owner married her, but when she got pregnant with Kyle by accident and couldn't work anymore, he fired her and got a divorce. He told her that if she tried to get money out of him, he would get custody of Kyle. Mom worked as a waitress at a bunch of different clubs around town, and got pregnant by a loser boyfriend who left her. The second son, my brother Randy, is illegitimate. Then once again, Mom went looking for love in all the wrong places and thought she found it in a successful married man who promised to leave his wife and marry her. She went so far as to tell his wife about their relationship to break them up, which it did, but the man didn't marry Mom anyway. He did give her a third child, my sister Tonya."

"Dad met Mom at a bar where she was waiting tables. He was very polite, Mom says, and asked if he could take her to a movie on her night off. He acted like a gentleman and never tried to get fresh. He wasn't going to mistreat a woman after what his own mother suffered. Mom liked him a lot and he was crazy about her. He didn't care anything about her past, since his wasn't so pure either. She was still a really beautiful woman with a great figure, even after having three children. They dated for just one month and he proposed. Dad adopted Kyle, Randy and Tonya not long after I was born. They named me John Kincade Monroe, with Mom's maiden name."

"Dad once worked on a construction job for a real estate broker who flipped houses. The broker was making big bucks at it, so Dad wanted to do the same. He had four kids to support. So he got a license, went to work for a broker selling houses and eventually became a broker himself. He quit the real estate agency he worked for and started flipping houses, doing all of the renovations himself in the beginning. He did really well and so did all of his children. The family owns a huge amount of real estate in the parish and surrounding areas."

"What Dad and Mom found out was that successful people who lived like respectable citizens were accepted as though they never had a past. Because a whole lot of people in this town have a shady past, too. Huh! This is New Orleans, after all. The town was built by pirates, smugglers, river rats, prisoners, prostitutes and European outcasts. Think about all the elected officials from around here who are in prison today!"

"So that's my family. An embezzler, a bigamist, a housemaid, a murderer, a stripper, a home-wrecker and two illegitimate siblings." Jack sat quietly for a minute to let Rose think about it. "Are you too ashamed of my family to marry *me*, Rose?"

"No," she said softly. "I would be very proud to marry you and make *your* family *my* family." He put the engagement ring back on her finger.

"This is what I think. The rest of the world knows you as a wealthy woman from a fine old New Orleans family and the godchild of the late great Eric Weber, who cared for you deeply. You will be loved and admired by everyone as a philanthropist and champion of the poor and homeless. The world knows me as a partner in a prestigious law firm, the son of a well-established family with large property holdings in the area. We are respectable upper class citizens of this city. We should tell Mom and Dad the truth just in case someone from the past shows up, so they won't be surprised. Dad is a very big guy and he would convince them in no uncertain terms that they were … um … *mistaken*? "

"Of course," said Rose with a chuckle.

"So, let's do this like respectable citizens are supposed to," Jack said, drawing Rose to her feet and holding her in his arms. "It's Saturday afternoon, so they're hearing confessions at St.

Louis Cathedral right now. It's been many years for me and I guess for you, too." Rose nodded. "We'll go to church and have the past washed away forever. We'll go to Mass together tomorrow and every Sunday. You're a virtuous Catholic school girl, after all, so we won't sleep together until we're married by the bishop at the cathedral."

"We won't??" Rose was disappointed at that.

"No. You'll walk down the aisle in virginal white and blush modestly on our wedding night." Rose laughed at that.

"Okay," she said. "Eric told me to behave like a lady when he left, and I did until I met you. So I promise to blush. But let's not wait too long, because I really, really like making love with you and I don't know how long I can hold out."

"If we rush it, people may think you're pregnant," he said, pretending to be scandalized.

"Let the old ladies count on their fingers. Our first baby will be born nine months after the wedding day. Then we'll start filling up our empty bedrooms with all the children you could want."

"We'll have beautiful little girl babies like their mother," he said. "At least half a dozen. That would fill up six empty bedrooms and still leave one for the Nanny and one guest room."

"No boy babies?" she asked.

"Nooo, boys are rough and noisy and dirty. And I would be jealous because you would love them too much. Let's just have sweet little girlie girls in pink dresses that I can spoil rotten. I'll buy them each a pony and they'll be debutants and spend their junior year abroad, mingling with royalty. I don't suppose I can spoil *you*, now, since you're richer than I am," he said with a laugh. "But

I can give you and our children my whole life. All
that I have and all that I am. I can love you alone
until the day I die."

232

CHAPTER 43

Sixteen-year-old Caroline ran from her bedroom, down the stairs, screaming for her mother. "Help, Mama, help me! Daddy's going to kill me!" She found Rose in the great room and hid behind her for protection. Jack was in hot pursuit down the stairs, but was stopped when Rose held her arms out to keep him away from Caroline.

"What's the problem, Honey?" she asked Jack calmly, putting her arms around his neck.

"I swear I'm going to kill that child," he said sneering at his eldest. He glared at Caroline over Rose's shoulder.

"You'll have to wait until tomorrow to kill her," Rose said. "We don't have time to dispose of the body before we meet Amy and Wizard and the rest of the gang for their anniversary dinner."

Rose turned to Caroline. "Give me your phone," she commanded with a scowl. Caroline sheepishly handed it over and Rose tucked it into the breast pocket of Jack's suit coat.

"Go to your room and stay there until breakfast," she said to Caroline.

"When can I get my phone back?" Caroline asked.

"When you can convince your father that you are truly sorry for whatever it was you did."

Katherine, daughter number two, was stomping down the stairs in a huff as Caroline was going up. She was still wearing her dirty soccer uniform and had grass in her hair. Holding out a multi-colored plastic disk to show her parents, she asked, "Do you know what this used to be? My bracelet. That little snot sister of mine melted it in her Easy Bake oven." The snot sister was seven-year-old Rebecca.

"We will make Becky pay you for it out of her allowance, okay?" Jack said patiently, kissing her on the forehead. "You can buy one exactly like it and lock it up in your jewelry box next time."

Two-year-old Elizabeth, daughter number four, came crying from the kitchen and reached for her daddy to hold her. He pink dress was smeared with the remains of her supper. The sash that normally tied in a bow at the back of the dress was missing one side, with the other half dragging on the floor behind her. Her dark curly hair had a chunk missing in the front where she tried to give herself a haircut earlier.

"What's the matter, Babycakes?" he said, cuddling her close.

"Kiddy bite me," she sobbed, showing her father the little red spot on her finger. It wasn't really a bite at all, but it scared her. Precious and Handsome were elderly cats now and had tolerated the children and their friends patiently for years. They had earned the right to be left in peace and to get grouchy when anyone disturbed their rest.

"Must be a good tasting finger!" he said, taking the tiny finger in his mouth and pretending to gobble it noisily. Elizabeth squealed.

"Nanna!" he called out for the live-in babysitter. "It's time for Elizabeth to get a bath. She smells like she's been in the litter box again," he laughed, handing his baby over with a kiss on her cheek.

When Jack and Rose were alone again, they went upstairs to change for their dinner out with their long-time friends and clients.

Amy, Albert and Jack and their respective spouses socialized together often, but Amy and Rose became especially close as they began having kids. The children became friends, too, since they were practically raised together and attended the same Catholic schools.

Amy and Wizard Laurent had four handsome blond sons so far and the Monroes had four beautiful brunette daughters. Both mothers thought it would be great if they were related by marriage someday. What a gene pool that would make! Beauty queens and geniuses!

"What's the problem with Caroline this time?" Rose asked him as she stripped down to her white silk bra and lace panties in their bedroom. Jack looked at his watch to see if they had time for a quickie. They didn't. Even though Rose had given birth four times, her figure was as hot as ever. She worked out in her gym downstairs to keep it that way. And Jack never got tired of admiring it and wanting her like they were newlyweds.

"Let's put an ad in the paper," he said with an exasperated sigh as he flopped down on the bed. "Horrible child, free to a good home."

Rose sat on the bed beside him to remove her stockings. She glanced at the clock next to the bed to see if there was time for a quickie. There wasn't. She hopped out of bed and went to collect a sexy dress and heels from her closet.

"Give her away like a stray cat? No way! You wouldn't want some other man to walk your beautiful baby down the aisle when she gets married, would you?"

"Married!" he said. "What man in his right mind would marry a smart-mouth, stubborn, bad-tempered girl like Caroline?"

"You did," she said with a shrug.

Other books by Cheryl Campos include:

The Grandparent Tree

Treasure

and

The Prince of River Road

All her titles are available from

Cheryl Campos
905 Highway 70 North
Rogersville, TN 37857

camposcheryl@charter.net

or

Amazon.com

www.ingramcontent.com/pod-product-compliance
Lightning Source LLC
Chambersburg PA
CBHW071406150726
48000CB00001B/180